JOKER

J.M. DABNEY

EXECUTIONERS BOOK 2

CONTENTS

Dedication

To all my readers who make it possible for me to tell my stories. Thank you all!

Special thanks to my amazing Beta Readers and Editor who put up with me and make my stories great.

Author's Note

This story contains scenes of a violent nature, mentions of rape and torture (All off page from characters pasts) and severe abuse. If you, as a reader, find this objectionable or triggering in any way, please be aware and don't read further.

1 Joker Could Make Lucifer Piss Himself

Sun shone bright, birds chirped, and Jackson Webb hated every second of it. He crossed his muscled arms across his chest. He watched Deputy Wren Gramble-Trenton with an arched, pierced brow. The man's jaw clenched in frustration as Wren stared at him. As even tempered as Wren was, the man had one hell of a temper Wren hid pretty well.

Wren was a little above average height, had a stocky frame, but the man was downright beautiful. Model perfection from his perfect dark hair to the tip of his uniform shoes. He liked the guy. Wren was married to Hunter and Linus Trenton, how they made that threesome shit work, boggled his damn mind.

"Joker, come on, don't fight me on this."

"I didn't do nothing." If he were the smiling type, he'd have grinned at his own lie.

He didn't regret what he did, and given the chance, he'd do it again. One warning seemed generous when it came to that fucker. No one put their hands on a woman, especially not in his presence. Ghost, Harper's husband, would've done the same. No one fucked with his best friend, Harper, on his watch. She didn't do anything to anybody. Just because she wasn't born in the right body didn't give someone the right to make her feel less than. He didn't care if the stupid fucker was new in town or not.

"You sent a man to the hospital."

"He didn't listen to me." Which was true enough.

"He barely put a fingertip on Harper."

"I told him not to touch her, he didn't listen, so I broke the finger."

Okay, he'd broken more than one finger, but, fuck, they'd heal. It wasn't like he'd broken the bastard's neck like he'd wanted to do.

Wren's lips twitched. It paid that one of his friends was married to a cop.

Maybe not, Wren reached for his cuffs.

"Harper and Ghost are on call to post bail."

Fuck, he hated when his best friends had to come bail him out. It wasn't like no one knew he was an asshole. He was broken, damaged goods. He always had this theory that he wasn't meant to be born. Someone, as fucked up as him, should've barely been a footnote, and he shouldn't have survived to make everyone around him miserable.

He clenched his back teeth. He was tired of everyone trying to fix him or thinking they knew what was best for him. Knowing what and who he was, were the first steps in accepting the shit he couldn't change.

"I got a job waiting for me. And Killer needs to eat. Come get me in a few hours."

"Joker, don't make this harder than it has to be."

He pointed at Wren. "I gave that fucker fair warning. I showed restraint."

"How did you—"

"First, I told him not to look at her or I'd take his fucking eyes out, but I only broke his finger."

"You know you—"

"Yeah, yeah, you going to arrest me or not, Wren?"

"Put out your hands, I know you ain't gonna give me your back. We gotta play this by the rules, you know Pelter doesn't play. He's strict and doesn't deviate from the book."

He just held out his hands and let Wren cuff him. He looked around at the crowd that had started to gather. He tilted his head as one spectator, in particular, caught his attention. The guy was one of those men that drew attention just by being. People like that pissed him off. The man's blue eyes shimmered with laughter, and one corner of his lush lips was pulled into a half-smile.

A rumble rolled up from deep in his chest.

"Joker, behave."

"I wasn't doing nothing."

He didn't bother giving Wren his attention. He continued to glare at the stranger. The bastard didn't pay him one bit of attention, just stood there with that fucking smile on his face. He hated being made fun of or belittled. He'd admit it to anyone, he was crazy, not stupid.

"Exactly."

"Can we get this freak show over, I got to get back to work. Doesn't my chariot await and all that bullshit?" He jerked his head around to Wren.

"Asshole." Wren chuckled and shook his head.

"That's nothing new."

Wren opened the door for him, and he slid into the back seat. He turned his gaze back to the gorgeous brunet leaning against the front of Heidi's Diner. He snarled as the man raised his hand and waved.

"Don't even think about killing Dem."

"Would I do that?"

"Your penchant for violence is legendary."

"Who's Dem?"

He knew who Dem was, but decided to pretend to be clueless, Ghost and Harper talked about the man all the time. Dem this, Dem that, they made it out like the man was a saint. There wasn't anyone in existence that was as perfect as they appeared.

He rarely paid attention to anyone or gave many people a second thought. The stories he'd heard about Dem fascinated him. He understood there were happy people in the world and he'd briefly studied the picture Ghost had of Dem on his mantle. The man had rainbow streamers on a pair of arm crutches, a big red clown nose, and even from the picture, it was clear the man was laughing.

"Demetri Urban."

"Ghost's friend?"

"Yeah, he's staying with Ghost and Harper for a while, working as a cook for Heidi. I'm surprised the amount of time you spend out at Ghost and Harper's place you haven't met him yet."

He didn't like strangers, so he'd avoided going out to Ghost's farm. He didn't like the way the picture of Demetri made him feel and the more distance between them, the better. Also, his best friends were newly married, they needed their space. They didn't need people hanging around while they got their shit together.

4

He leaned his head back and closed his eyes, he'd slept better since Harper gave him a puppy. At five months old, she was a badass beast at almost three pounds. He normally kept Killer in his hoodie pocket, but today he'd left her at home. He wouldn't admit it to anyone, but he missed her.

She liked their motorcycle rides best from her spot in his backpack. The micro dog turned out to be the best and only present he had ever been given. He'd put up a bit of a fight when Harper gave Killer to him, but he snatched her as quickly as possible and hid her away in his hoodie pocket. Putting distance between Harper and Ghost in case they gave her to him and then tried to take her away. He hated that he thought that way about his friends, but he hadn't wanted to take the chance.

The trip to the building that housed the Sheriff's department took no more than ten minutes, and he opened his eyes as Wren stopped the cruiser. Wren came around the vehicle, opened the door, and thankfully the man didn't touch him. He was getting tired of his skin crawling. The rage that always simmered right below the surface was ready to explode. He slipped from the back seat and headed for the front doors. They'd let him go—they always did.

Joker never meant to get angry, it just happened. It had been that way his entire life. He didn't doubt he was broken since his mother got pregnant. Everyone around there knew what he was—a product of rape. His mother, Mary, from what he remembered, was a sweet and beautiful girl, soft spoken and selfless. His father had taken away her innocence at thirteen. Her obsessively devout parents forced her to marry her rapist.

His mother never told him, he hadn't known until after she'd disappeared when he was eight, and four years later, he had found her journals. She'd loved him though, wrote it on the faded pages, mixed in with things she'd dreamed about, and knew she'd never have. The nightmares were there as well, every demeaning and horrendous act she'd endured at the hands of his father made clear in black ink on lined pages.

She was twenty-one when she'd left, they said she'd packed up and just took off in the middle of the night. He'd known different. She never would've left him with his evil bastard of a father. He knew his father had killed her. No one had listened to him after he learned of the Hell his mother went through, and he'd told or tried to tell Sheriff Thorpe at the time. No one stepped in when he couldn't hide the bruises or whip marks, he lost count of broken bones and stitches before his fifteenth birthday.

And then he'd—

"What the hell is he doing here," Sheriff Camden Pelter hollered through his open office door.

Sheriff Pelter was dark skinned and massive, his shoulders would easily fill a doorway. They'd learned he was Scary's cousin, one of the owners of Brawlers Bar outside town. The two men didn't look alike except for their size. Pelter was dark where Scary was lighter, and Pelter looked ten years younger than his mid-forties.

He liked Pelter. The man was fair and didn't seem to overlook the small-minded bullshit in Powers, but being the first black Sheriff in town couldn't be easy when some of the so-called upstanding citizens hated the man got the job.

Thorpe had let shit go without even a slap on the wrist too easily. The man's nephew had tortured Harper for years, and everyone knew about it. Stopping it had ended in Bill taking his last breath. He didn't and wouldn't regret he'd protected Harper, no matter what anyone thought of him. The more people who thought he was dangerous, the fewer people he had to deal with.

"You told me to bring him in."

"When have you ever listened to me?"

Joker was amused, but he knew it didn't show.

"You cuffed him? Why did you…screw it, take them off and bring him in here."

He held out his hands for Wren to remove the cuffs.

"I know you're laughing at me."

"Would I do that, Wren?"

"You so fucking would. Go on."

He nodded and ambled across the room and stepped into Pelter's office, and closed the door behind him. Pelter leaned on the edge of the desk. He didn't like when people stood over him, so he stayed standing with his back against the door.

"What the hell am I going to do with you, Joker," Pelter asked as the larger man folded his arms over his massive chest.

"Let me go."

"Listen, I've read your files and your—"

He knew what Pelter was going to say, and he didn't want to hear it. He'd left that shit behind sixteen years ago when he'd stepped out of prison.

"He's not my anything."

"Fine, I've read it all. You were charged as an adult in your—his death. Why it wasn't ruled justifiable, I don't know because if a case ever called for dismissal, it was yours. I just can't have you running around town acting as a vigilante. Thorpe is dead, I'm the Sheriff now. I won't let things go or overlook them. You don't have to be a one-man army to take out every abusive significant other, or bigot in town. I need you to let me do my job."

"You're doing a shit one."

"Joker." Pelter groaned and scrubbed his hands over his face.

"Thorpe may be dead, but his rules are still applying. Every bastard who thinks they can put their hands on women and children are still feeling like they're bulletproof. Every bigot still believes they can vandalize someone's home, business or can jump them when they're minding their own business."

"Please just let me handle things, Joker. It's hard enough trying to prove I'm different than Thorpe. It's like a fucking nightmare."

"I won't make promises."

"I didn't think you would. Get out."

He didn't wait to be dismissed again, he surged away from the door, threw it open and headed for the nearest exit. He had a job waiting for him, and Killer would be ready for her dinner. She liked her routine just like him, it kept him focused on something other than his past and the nightmares. Because Garnet Webb may be dead, but he was alive and well in his head.

2 Tell Me More

The man was too damn gorgeous to be so cranky, Demetri Urban thought as he studied the picture of Jackson Webb that he'd moved from the mantle to the coffee table. Okay, he was feeling a bit stalker-ish but who could blame him. Jackson was physical perfection. He wasn't shallow in the least. Others might not find the snarling man attractive, but Dem wanted to cuddle Jackson—preferably naked.

He'd been warned it was a bad idea, yet it didn't change the urge. Seeing him earlier while Wren arrested Jackson sealed the deal. Jackson wore this little half smile that would probably terrify normal people—good thing he wasn't normal. Nowhere near.

"You're like some teenage girl with a crush," Gideon's amused voice came from behind him.

He didn't look away from the picture.

"Should I write him a love note? Ask him to circle yes or no if he wants to go steady?"

"Dem, I wouldn't put it passed you."

Gideon sat down beside him, and Dem leaned to the side to rest his head on Gideon's shoulder. The handsome redhead had been his friend for almost ten years—since the first time Gideon had employed him as a caterer for Gideon's event company.

He was exhausted. The kitchen at Heidi's Diner was busy as fuck. It was a one-person operation so different from his former team back in New York. It was harder and more stressful to maneuver with his arm crutches, and by the end of the night, his hips and thighs ached to the point he needed to take one of his pain pills.

He wouldn't complain though, he was healthy except for his dodgy hip joints and pelvis. He worked out enough to keep the bone degeneration at a minimum, but that wasn't a guarantee for his future. So many surgeries had damaged the bone that he didn't know how much longer before he might need more corrective action. He didn't know if he wanted to go under the knife again. He was damn tired of hospitals and too many doctors with excuses of *we just don't know.*

His parents hadn't treated him different growing up. Whatever he wanted to do, he was encouraged and never told he couldn't, at least not by his parents.

He was tired of thinking about his aching body and wanted more pleasant things to think about. "Tell me more about him."

"Dem."

Gideon's tone held a clear warning, but Jackson was Gideon's friend, one of his best from what he'd heard. Why couldn't he have an interest in the man? Even if that interest wasn't returned, everyone needed a friend, no one ever had enough of those.

"Don't Dem me. Tell me more."

"Joker—"

"Jackson."

He hated when they called Jackson Joker, he had a perfectly sexy name to go with the bad boy image, why not use it?

"I can already see having you come stay here was a mistake."

"Don't be mean."

"Jo—Jackson doesn't like anybody really except Harper, everyone else he tolerates."

"He looks hot in handcuffs."

"Please never say that again. You, Jackson and handcuffs is a visual I don't need. Dem, I'm serious, never touch Joker. Never come up behind him. His fight instinct is strong."

"He just needs some good loving and some cuddles."

"I'm serious. Joker hasn't had the easiest life, and that's an understatement. He's one of my best friends, but he is not your type."

"I'm almost forty, let me be the judge of that."

Forty was a couple years away, but it was close enough. He didn't act his age, didn't want to miss an opportunity in life with doubts and what ifs. Life was meant to be lived to the fullest before it was gone in the blink of an eye. Tomorrow wasn't a guarantee, he didn't want to wake up in the morning and regret he didn't take a chance—grab onto an opportunity.

Gideon sighed. "Don't say I didn't warn you."

"I won't."

"I'm off to join my beautiful wife in bed. You need help to your room?"

Anyone else and he'd be offended by that question, but Gideon was there the day the doctors told him he'd need to rely on arm crutches. His friend only wanted to help.

"No, I'm going to sit here for a bit. I'm still on New York time. It's making the new day job hell."

"No more five a.m. bedtime for you."

Gideon kissed his forehead, and he smiled as his friend patted his thigh. He straightened to let Gideon up and sunk back into the thick cushions.

"Goodnight, Dem."

"You too."

He waited until he was alone to let his mind wander to what made him take a working vacation in a small Georgia town. He had been with his ex for two years, and the relationship was great. They didn't argue any more than any other couple. They had sex regularly, but it seemed more like a requisite requirement. Okay, the sex wasn't even vanilla, it had no flavor at all. His ex was just too serious. Fun wasn't in Aiden's vocabulary. He needed silly. Needed to be able to laugh.

Aiden didn't possess that kind of simple joy in life. It sucked the life from him. Unfortunately, when you dated your boss, a breakup left you unemployed as well. He didn't mind losing his job. He didn't mind taking a semi-vacation to stay with Gideon and Harper. Going where life took him was just something he did.

He'd been born with a deformity of the hips and pelvis, surgery was done to correct it, but nothing worked forever. After he'd quit growing, they performed another surgery, and he had more metal in his hips and pelvis than bone. Growing up, the reconstruction worked, gave him normal ability to walk, running wasn't his specialty but who the fuck loved to run?

The degeneration of the surrounding bone started in his late twenties and would worsen as he got older, he was a pro at working a kitchen. He'd found a system that worked for him.

There was something he was positive about. He trusted in his gut, and it told him Jackson Webb needed him. Over the past few weeks, he'd studied Jackson from the window of his kitchen.

Jackson always sat in booth six, his back to the wall with a full view of the front door and all exits. He ordered six pancakes, with tons of butter, but always went light on the syrup. Which in his opinion was the best part of pancakes, downing them in warm, sticky syrup. Jackson had exactly three cups of black, unsweetened coffee. Every morning, seven days a week, but he only saw Jackson five days a week. Since Heidi gave him weekends off.

He'd been waiting for Jackson to come out to the farm, but the man continued to make himself scarce. He needed to get the man's attention. How the hell was he supposed to do that when he knew Jackson avoided the farm because he was there?

He dug his phone out from under his thigh, unlocked it, and he hit the speed dial for his mom.

"You better tell me you're in Vegas getting married if you're calling me at four a.m."

He snorted at his mother's disgruntled sleepy voice.

"I have to get the man to notice me first, Ma."

He held the phone away from his ear as his mom screamed like a teenage girl. Gretchen Urban was like Super Mom. She never let anything get her down. He'd learned early, he'd gotten his personality from her.

Now, he loved his Da, but Cliff Urban was a total curmudgeon. It was beyond cute seeing his stoic and cranky dad cater to his wife's every whim. Last year, Gretchen wanted to live and tour Europe, and Cliff made it happen even as he complained the entire way.

"Gretchen, do you know what damn time it is?"

"Shut up, dear, our son has a crush. Oh, we haven't had crush conversations in forever."

"Better than the one he spent the last two years with?"

"I don't know, I'm going to make coffee, go back to sleep."

He smiled as he listened to masculine grumbling and then the bed creaked.

"So, tell me about this boy?"

"I don't think he's much of a boy, maybe my age."

"Mature, good, does he at least have a sense of humor."

"I don't know. I haven't talked to him yet, but, Ma..." He dragged out the last word for like twenty syllables. "He's so hot in handcuffs."

"Nice, what else?" His mother gasp was followed by a long pause. "You didn't hook up and not exchange info? Please tell me you were safe."

"What about me having not talked to him yet didn't you get? He was being arrested."

"Son."

"Don't, he stood up for one of his best friends. She was being harassed, he took care of the situation, and he was picked up for it."

"Aw, that's so sweet. So, what's the problem?"

"He's a bit cranky. Gideon told me he didn't have the easiest time growing up."

"Then treat him like I did your father."

"Um, Ma, didn't Da kidnap you and leave you in the middle of nowhere?"

He resisted the urge to laugh, his mother had recounted the story so many times over the years while his father snapped his paper and rolled his eyes. His mother, a free-spirited young woman of eighteen, and his father almost ten years her senior.

Cliff had worked for her father for several years as a ranch hand. As soon as she'd turned eighteen, she went on a single-minded hunt for her prey. His father put up with it for a whole Summer waiting for her to go away to college, but finding his lingerie clad boss' daughter in his bed was the last straw. He hogtied her and took her to the farthest border of the ranch and left her. Only thirty minutes passed before his father was back and the rest was history. They'd been together ever since.

"It was just his way of flirting, son, he did come back for me."

"Yes, he did. But I'm not hog-tying Jackson or wearing lingerie."

"Then be boring about it and ask him on a date."

"Easier said than—"

"We didn't raise you with a defeatist attitude, Demetri."

"Yes, ma'am."

"You'll figure it out. So, tell me how everything's going in your new home."

He settled in to catch up with his mother, but at the back of his mind, he plotted how to make Jackson Webb his.

3 This Isn't What He Ordered

A new waitress was working, he didn't know her name and hadn't bothered to ask. As long as she got his order right, he didn't care. He laid his silverware out just so, turned his empty mug handle to the right, and waited for his usual breakfast to arrive, along with his coffee refill.

Heidi knew what he wanted without asking. She just wrote the ticket when she saw him come in, put it in the window, and came over to fill his coffee mug. No chit chat, no inane questions such as *how are you*, people didn't like to hear *pissed off as usual*.

He started counting as his irritation grew. By the time he finished his first mug of coffee, his breakfast was normally there. He glanced up as he heard sneakers squeak on the floor. The girl set his plate down on the table, and he glared at it. A huge smiley face disfigured the top of his perfect stack of pancakes.

"What the fuck is this?"

"Um, your breakfast, Dem said—"

He surged from the booth, stormed to the kitchen, and he punched open the door.

"Hello, Jackson." A smiling man leaned against the wall with his arms crossed.

"You—"

"Everyone calls me Dem, but you would know that if you visited your best friends."

"You fucked up my breakfast, it's a simple fucking order."

The man didn't even blink, just kept smiling with that perky little lift to the corners of his mouth. He didn't like being made fun of, and he clenched his fists at his sides.

"You didn't like your morning smile, Jackson?"

"Stop calling me that."

"It's your name, and it's a very sexy name."

He growled deep in his chest, his fist connected with the steel cooler door, and he spun on his toes. He slammed through the swinging door and the diner, then out the front door.

"Joker, you okay," his friend, King's voice barely broke through his anger.

"Yeah, I'm fine. I have to get to work."

"Isn't it time for your break—"

He didn't wait to hear the end of the question and made the ten-minute walk to his shop. When he threw open the sliding doors, the scent of motor oil and rubber filled his nose. His stomach growled, and he ignored it, lunch was only four hours away. He could make it. He'd gone hungrier a lot longer than a few hours. Garnet starved him for almost a week, and he'd survived.

A tiny growling bundle of fur bounded into his garage. He scooped Killer up and shoved her into the pocket of his hoodie, and her little head popped up through the hole he'd cut in the top. He rubbed her ears between his thumbs and index fingers. Her tiny little rumbles threatening, well, as threatening as less than three pounds of dog could get.

She settled in and let him pet her. She knew when he needed extra time. She needed her routine as much as he did. He'd had a pet once before his mother disappeared. After that, it had gone missing one night, just like his mother had. Everything he loved disappeared. He'd never had anything of his own, making him possessive of his job, his home, his garage, and Killer. He didn't expect anything else to remain, but those things were his.

His stomach rumbled again, but he shook his head. He had one peanut butter sandwich and one bottle of water, that was all he'd have for lunch. Nothing more.

"Hi."

He spun as that man's voice sounded behind him. No one came up behind him without announcing their presence. Everyone knew that, and the man should've been warned. A white plastic to-go bag was wrapped around the man's wrist, while his hands wrapped around the arm crutch handles.

"What's that?"

"Pancakes, no smiley face, lots of butter, a small cup of syrup."

"Why?"

Dem grimaced, and he looked embarrassed. "My flirting apparently didn't go well."

"Why the fuck were you flirting? Are you desperate?"

"No, here, eat your breakfast."

The man held out the bag with his right hand, the crutch dangled there. Ghost said Dem had a degenerative disease or something. He didn't know all the details, and he'd barely listened, he'd just helped with a few things to make the house more accessible to Ghost's friend.

He took quick steps forward, grabbed the bag and retreated before the man could touch him. Touch meant pain and humiliation, he wouldn't set himself up for it.

"Um, what's that?"

He studied Dem pointing and looked down to see Killer staring just as hard as he was at Dem.

"Killer."

"Oh, is that Tiny's sister," Dem asked with a bright smile.

The smile was better than the cringe from earlier. He liked the way the man lit up when he was happy. It was odd because he didn't pay much attention to people's emotions. Some had mood swings drastic enough to change the weather, and he found it exhausting to keep up. He had boredom and rage, simple enough.

"Yeah."

Dem reached forward. "May I?"

He stepped back. "No."

"Okay. I better get back to work, I locked up and put a sign on the door."

"You can't—"

"I called Heidi and told her I had to bring you breakfast. You should know the hour you come in to have breakfast is the deadest time of the day."

"You didn't—"

"I did, I shouldn't have teased you. Can I buy you dinner to make up for it?"

"No."

Dem seemed to deflate, but what he assumed was confusion was present in the man's features. Some things he could pick out and others he was clueless.

"Okay, I better get going, it was nice seeing you again, Jack—Joker."

He frowned and his brow furrowed at the—sadness. Maybe that was it. He'd seen Harper sad, he'd even remembered his mother crying when he was a boy, but he'd never seen someone sad because he told them no. Fuck, no one had asked him on a date before, it wasn't a date, *a sorry for making fun of him meal.*

"I don't like to be made fun of; to be made to feel stupid. Don't do it again."

"I'm very sorry, Joker."

He nodded and waited for the man to leave, but instead, Dem headed toward him. He noticed the man's left foot dragged. This wasn't the—he caught Dem as the man's toes caught on a hose on the floor. He caught Dem's biceps and held on, the man's breathing ragged and his face slightly pale.

"Could I sit for a minute? I tired myself out walking over here. I'm sorry."

He released Dem and grabbed his grease-stained stool, and set it behind Dem. He stepped back and started to nervously rub Killer's ears again. He didn't like people in his space—touching his things.

"Why haven't you been out to the farm since I moved here?"

Fuck, a minute ago he had an unwanted guest, and he changed into a chatty unwanted guest. Wasn't Dem warned about him? Stay away. Felon. Insane person. Violent bastard.

"I don't like strangers."

"Well, we've met so you can come back out."

"Okay."

A tiny smile that held no warmth tilted the corners of Dem's mouth. "You're lying. Gideon warned me about your Joker-speak."

"Shouldn't you be getting back to work?"

"Trying to get rid of me?"

"Yes."

"You don't spare people's feelings, do you?"

"No."

"Fuck, it's like pulling teeth."

He watched Dem use his arm crutches to get to his feet, and the man spun to head for the door.

"Eat your breakfast, it's probably cold, but you need it. Your stomach has been growling for the last five minutes. I don't like that you were going to go hungry because of me."

He opened his mouth to say something, anything, but Dem left without a backward glance or another word. His friends worried about him. They made sure they were always available if he needed bail, but no one had ever wondered if he was hungry or worried if he was.

Killer nipped at his fingers when she was done with his attention. He leaned over to pick up the bag he'd dropped and took the seat Dem just vacated. He frowned at the urge to go after the man to see if he needed a ride but shook it off. He rested the to-go box on his knees, Killer shifted until her head stuck out the left side of the pocket. He broke off a tiny piece off the top pancake and fed her the bite, then another until she turned away from another offering.

Once he knew she was full and content, he drizzled the tiny amount of syrup over them and ate the butter soaked lukewarm pancakes. He forced himself not to eat too quickly. No one was there to take away his food.

Garnet wasn't there to let him eat just so much, not enough to fill his stomach, and then snatch the plate away.

He remembered the days he wouldn't be allowed anything but peanut butter on stale bread. One cup of water. As a grown man, his lunch was a reminder.

He secretly longed for something sweet. Cakes and cookies, pastries that his friend, Ben, made at his bakery, but it was a luxury he couldn't afford. Something he refused to get used to.

He wouldn't admit it to anyone, but his friends made him jealous. They had men who loved them. He observed the sweetness of touches, the loving tilt of smiles sometimes small or wide when their men appeared. Dem had smiled at him earlier. Called him by his name and said it was sexy. He wondered what it would be like if it wasn't made in jest.

Anger burned in his chest, his food became lodged in his throat as he launched his breakfast against the nearest wall. Killer didn't react, too used to his outbursts. He sat frozen on the uncomfortable stool and stared off into space. Emotions other than rage were unacceptable, and his anger settled the abnormal urges. He wasn't like Psycho, Ghost, Bull, or any of the other men he was friends with. He wasn't normal. He was broken. His existence a cruelty he suffered. His penance for being what and who he was, he was a monster just as the animal who forced him into being.

4 How Was He Supposed to Get Jackson's Attention?

Dem leaned back against the kitchen counter and listened to Gideon and Harper upstairs. Harper giggled, and he smiled at Gideon's answering laugh. Those two were like the perfect couple. They had the relationship he'd always wanted, very much like his parents. They doted on each other. He rarely came in from work and didn't see Gideon and Harper cuddled up, kissing or sometimes just holding hands.

He loved his friends, but they made him feel inadequate, something he'd never experienced before. His love life hadn't ever been what he'd wanted it to be. His boyfriends were always too serious and never affectionate with him.

Groaning, he let his head fall back and realized Jackson was—no, there was something about the man. He even liked Jackson's bluntness. He sensed Jackson's life was horrific, a lot more than people knew. The man's nervous tics, the anxiousness that caused Jackson to rub Killer's ears when he was uneasy. It was kind of cute how he used his puppy as a security blanket.

Now he sounded like an asshole. He'd learned a few things. Jackson didn't like to be teased. Touching was completely off limits.

Touch was important for developing intimacy, but it was dead as an option.

How was he going to get Jackson's attention?

The man was immune to his immeasurable charm. He knew a lot of men didn't want to date a partner with a disability. Although he'd never let that get him down, it still sucked when men liked him just fine when he was sitting, but his arm crutches turned them off. Sometimes he thought the only reason his ex dated him was to keep him around as a chef. His name had drawn customers over the five years he'd worked at Aiden's place.

He raised one hand to run his fingers through his long hair, the waves tangled around his fingers. He considered himself handsome, not the best looking, and at almost forty, he still had a youthful face. His upper body was powerful, but his legs had withered over the last few years. He made sure he worked enough to keep them strong enough to bear his weight although, he didn't know how much longer that would be. His days were numbered in the kitchen. He knew he'd work out a way, he always did; he just wasn't ready to have to adapt again, yet.

For now, all he wanted was a chance with Jackson. One date, hell, he'd settle for one conversation—just a chance to listen to the gruffness of his voice. He swore the man could make anything sound dirty.

He reached for his phone on the counter behind him. He scrolled through his contacts and found Jackson's number. So he may have searched Gideon's phone for Jackson's contact information. Could stalker be added to his experience list on his resume? He slipped his arm crutches back on his forearms and made his way to the downstairs bedroom they'd given him.

He flopped onto the bed and connected the call, he listened to the rings. After the fifth one, he was about to hang up.

"What," Jackson barked in his ear.

"You have charming phone etiquette, Jackson."

He moved his crutches to lean them against the nightstand as he shifted to get comfortable.

"Who the fuck is this?"

"Dem. I wanted to make sure you ate."

"You called me at ten at night to make sure I ate breakfast?"

Jackson's tone conveyed clearly the man thought him insane. It was like banging his head against the wall repeatedly and expecting to get a different result on the next crash. All he was going to end up with was a migraine.

"Yeah, so?"

"Bored, city boy?"

He smiled, Jackson hadn't hung up on him...yet. It had to be a good sign.

"No, not bored. Is there something wrong with me checking on you?"

"Get in trouble for closing shop?"

Not the subtlest change of subject.

"No, apparently you're one of Heidi's best customers, but you're in trouble for wasting my morning masterpiece."

"Bullshit."

"So when can I take you out on a date?"

There was silence, he held his breath and waited, he pulled his phone away from his ear to check to make sure Jackson didn't hang up on him.

"Never."

"What are you doing now?"

"In bed."

Don't say anything inappropriate, don't say it. He bit the inside of his cheek. Being subtle wasn't in his nature, but he sensed Jackson need a lighter hand. Jackson didn't like being pushed or teased, he didn't like touch. This was going to be a nightmare trying to get his man. And no matter what Jackson thought, Jackson was his.

"Early day tomorrow?"

"Sorta, I gotta handle a few things tomorrow."

"Mysterious, I love that in a man."

He smiled at Jackson's huff but suppressed his need to laugh. Frustrating Jackson was going to become his favorite pastime.

"You're fucking annoying."

"I thought your name was Jackson and we ain't—"

"What is wrong with you? I swear if you're desperate for some dick there's plenty of it out at Brawlers. You could have your pick."

"I don't just want just someone's dick, Jackson, only a very particular—"

"You're not getting mine."

"How do you know? One date, Jackson, come on, you might actually have fun. I've been told I'm great company."

"I'll pick you on my bike Friday, be ready by 8, if you're late I pull away."

"O—" The other end of the conversation went silent, and he looked at his phone, Jackson had hung up on him. What the fuck, not a good night or anything. Damn man, then it registered, he had a date with Jackson. Unholy fuck, he had a date. He fist pumped the air and rolled from bed, and grabbed his crutches, and he moved as fast as they allowed.

"Gideon, I have a date, he said yes," he yelled as he moved through the house.

"What the fuck are you yelling about?" A shirtless Gideon appeared around the corner.

"He said yes, well, not yes, he told me to be ready Friday night, but I did ask him when we'd go on a date, so technically he said yes!"

"Who said yes?" Harper popped from behind Gideon.

"Jackson, he told me to be ready at eight, he'd be here on his...oh shit, he said bike. I can't ride a bike." He plopped down on the arm of the couch dejected.

He'd seen Gideon take Harper out plenty of times. She rested her feet on the pegs, but his legs weren't strong enough to keep them up that long. He tended to shift a lot to get comfortable. A motorcycle seat definitely wouldn't allow for that.

"I'm sure if you call him back, he'll bring his truck."

Harper was sweet, and he understood what Gideon saw in her.

"No, I don't...I'll figure something out."

"Dem, Joker's a bit of an asshole, but I'm sure if you just tell him you can't, then he'd figure something out." Harper smiled at him.

"He said he had an early day, I'll see about talking to him when he comes in for breakfast Monday."

"Hey, look at it like this, he said yes, and that's big. Joker doesn't volunteer to spend time with anyone and riding his bike gives you his back. That's unheard of."

He knew Harper was being nice and trying to cheer him up, but it just wasn't working.

"Why doesn't—"

"Um, how much have you heard about Joker," Gideon asked.

"Not much, no one really talks about him, why?"

"I'm just going to say this, Joker barely made it out of his teens with his sanity intact. Just take it easy, don't push him too much, and only touch him if he touches you first. And whatever you do, don't come up behind him without announcing it."

They kept telling him that, but wouldn't tell him why. He just wanted to know what he was up against. He hated feeling like this. His life hadn't been easy with a disability, but he'd worked with it, adapted to make his dreams come true. It was the first time he felt at a loss as to what to do.

"I better go to bed."

"Dem," Gideon said his name.

"It's fine, I'll figure something out, I always do."

He pushed up on his crutches and headed to bed. He'd always wanted to ride a motorcycle, he'd do it, but first, he had to talk to Jackson. He just hoped the man understood. Being reminded of his limitations pissed him off, yet it wouldn't last long—he hoped.

5 Fuck, Joker Had a Date

Friday night came around too quickly. Breakfast time at Heidi's had been unusually busy, so he luckily hadn't had to talk to Dem. It also made it impossible for him to back out. That wasn't going to happen, once he made a decision, he stuck with it. The next morning he'd had a thought…how would Dem ride behind him with his crutches? He figured it out, but he wondered what the man would think about it. Would Dem feel less than?

Most of his life he'd felt inadequate at being normal, so he'd given up on that bullshit. He didn't want anyone else to feel lacking, though.

He veered onto the long dirt driveway toward Ghost's place. One minute late and he'd leave, he'd already warned the man. Part of him was hoping Dem wouldn't be ready, and he could go back to his trailer for solo beers and movies.

He rolled to a stop beside Ghost's bike and kicked down his stand. He didn't get off right away. He tried to calm that edge of panic at having someone behind him. Garnet had always caught him with his back turned. The first brutal blow stunned him enough that he hadn't fought back. Instinct told him to hit first and ask questions later.

He gave his head a sharp shake and dismounted. He didn't really have anything appropriate for a date, so he'd worn his usual clothes. Jeans, black t-shirt, his favorite black hoodie, and his scuffed boots. He told himself to knock it off and jogged up the steps to the front door. The door opened before he could knock. Relief hit him when he saw Dem was dressed much like him except he wore a leather jacket over a navy-blue t-shirt.

"Hi, Jackson."

Dem smiled at him, and he started to protest the use of his first name. He had a feeling it wouldn't help. The man seemed to enjoy busting his balls.

"Dem. You ready?"

"Um—"

Dem looked off, he noticed the man's smile wasn't as bright as normal.

"What? You don't want to go?"

It was exactly what he'd wanted minutes before, but suddenly he was hurt it seemed the man wanted to back out.

"Yes," Dem yelled, then rolled his eyes. "It's just I can't ride—"

"Oh is that all, I got it covered, you ready?"

"Yes. Harper and Gideon made themselves scarce for some reason."

"They like to fuck in the greenhouse."

"Thanks for that information."

"You're welcome."

Dem smiled and shook his head.

He stepped to the side and Dem preceded him toward the bike. The man froze.

"What?"

"You changed your bike."

He'd only changed out the single seat with one for a passenger with a backrest.

"Temp shit, no big deal, I had to modify things a bit. Can you get on and off by yourself?"

"Yeah."

He didn't offer to help as Dem held onto both crutches with his right hand and used his left to lift his leg over. Once the man was settled, Dem's back against the rest, he stepped forward. He took lengths of Velcro from his saddlebags, then he lifted Dem's right foot to the peg. The knee was bent, and he wrapped the material completely around calf and thigh. It would give if necessary but would hold the man's legs up.

"Not too tight?"

"No, no, it's fine."

He glanced up to find Dem watching him; an odd emotion in his eyes. He ignored it and repeated on the other leg.

"Where do I put my crutches?"

"Right here," Joker said as he took the crutches, pulled Dem's left leg to the side and secured them in a crutch holder he'd modified for the bike. They snapped into two brackets for each crutch that held them in place. He'd tested it with a cane on a 70 mph ride a few nights ago. It had taken a lot of modifying to make everything work with the vintage frame of his custom motorcycle. It was the first one he'd built after he'd gotten out of prison at twenty-one.

"You didn't have to do all this for me."

"No big deal, it gave me something to do when I couldn't sleep. You ever ride before?"

"No."

"You're gonna scoot up behind me, wrap your arms around my waist and hold on. Don't fight into the turn. You'll throw us off balance. You follow my lead."

"Like dancing?"

"Don't know, never done it before."

"Dance or ride with someone else?"

"Ain't done either."

He thrust his helmet in Dem's direction and helped Dem put it on, then pulled a half-helmet out of his bag for himself.

He didn't want to talk about it anymore. The date was about scaring the man off. Dem wasn't for him. Hopefully, the smiling man would get it and leave him alone. He wasn't fit for anyone, especially not someone like Dem. He wasn't normal. He was rage-filled and broken.

He mounted the bike, then he waited until Dem followed his instructions. The man's chest against his back urged him to jerk away, to get off and put distance between them. He fought it, chose to start his bike and walked it backward, then headed off toward the main road. Instead of turning in the direction of town, he headed for Brawlers. The rough, gay biker bar was as unromantic as he could think of and it was also his kind of place.

Dem's fingers danced over his stomach, and he tensed until he forced himself to relax. His skin crawled as if bugs shimmied beneath his flesh. He was confident the man couldn't hurt him physically since he'd survived the worst that could be thrown at a man. His childhood memories were tainted by torture, sleep deprivation, and the pain of whip and blade. Each time more horrific than the last, desensitizing him to pain until Garnet upped the stakes. He had fingernails that had never fully grown back.

He clenched his jaw and pushed the past away, and just made the trip to their destination.

The flashing Brawlers sign came into view, and he pulled into the gravel parking lot. He rolled to a stop next to one of the owners' bikes. Scary and the rest of the Brawlers crew let their friends park up front.

He got off the bike, removed his helmet and then Dem's to reveal a bright smile and shimmering eyes. He looked away from the too handsome man. Dem wasn't pretty, his jaw was square and covered in stubble. Dem's body was powerfully built except for his legs, they were thin compared to the more developed muscles of his upper body and arms.

"I haven't been to Brawlers yet."

"Ghost and Harper don't spend much time here except for when Executioners play here." He spoke as he helped Dem remove the straps, dismounted, and he released the locks on the crutches.

He got the man settled. They slowly made their way to the front door. Crave, Head of Security, was posted at the door. The mammoth blond smiled.

"Hey, Joker, how ya doing, man?"

"Good."

"Who's your friend?"

"Crave, this is Dem, Ghost's friend."

He stood back as they shook hands, and he checked the area. It was an old habit, he never went anywhere without an escape plan.

"Ghost told us about you, but ain't brought you out here. Have fun tonight. Tell Twitch your first round is on me."

"Oh, man, I've heard about Twitch."

"My husband does have a reputation."

"Can I give him sugar and coffee," Dem asked.

He shot the man a look and saw Dem looking too excited by the prospect.

"No," he and Crave yelled.

"Oh, come on, I have to see it at least once."

"He's going home with me, man. Please, he gets in trouble, and he's a major little shit."

"But?"

Crave's grin turned wicked, and it made him uncomfortable.

"I do like making my boy pay, though."

"Thought so...so?"

"Still no."

"Damn," Dem pouted.

"Y'all have fun, and don't let me catch you giving my boy sugar or caffeine."

"Fine," Dem muttered and walked through the propped open doors.

"Keep an eye on your man tonight, Joker. We've already broken up a few fights."

"I got him handled."

"Just saying, man."

He followed Dem inside, the man was turned and waiting for him.

"Joker," Lucky's voice caught him off guard.

"Oh fuck," he muttered.

The tall, thin man with dreadlocks bounced over, his big brunet husband in tow. Priest looking at Lucky with such an expression of love that even a bastard like him could recognize it. Priest and Lucky were like the odd couple, but Lucky was infinitely devoted to his husband.

"Oh, you're on a date, you finally getting some D, my friend, shit, just wait until I tell Mama you're giving it to someone else."

"Lily is a fucking menace."

He observed Dem. The man's expression open and friendly, he radiated confidence. He didn't understand what Dem was doing there with him. Why the fuck did Dem even make an effort?

"You know you love my mama, you just won't give in. The bastard is rude, I'm Lucky, and this is my husband, Priest. You're new in town. You're the cook at Heidi's."

Priest said hello, but moved behind Lucky. Priest wasn't much on new people and crowds, so he stayed near Lucky unless they were in a group of their friends.

"Yeah, Dem, nice to meet you two."

"You're Ghost's friend."

"Still trips me out when I hear Gideon called Ghost."

"We all get nicknames."

"Yeah, how did you get yours?"

"I'm an accident waiting to happen, I'm lucky to be alive."

Dem laughed, and he narrowed his eyes. He didn't like that laugh, someone else had caused it—he growled. This was about scaring the man off. Not getting whatever he was over the man.

"Why do you all call Jackson Joker, I like his real name."

"Oh, he's a cranky fucker. If he smiles, he's ready to kill someone. So we had to find a name that was total opposite to fuck with him. So, Joker it was."

"Don't say that, he's so cute, though. Look at that scowl right there. Sexy as fuck."

"Man, where did you find this one? He might be crazier than me."

"We're going to the bar," he barked and placed his hand on Dem's lower back, urged him toward the bar at the back.

"It was nice meeting you two," Dem called over his shoulder.

The crowd parted when they saw him coming. Twitch noticed him and removed the reserved sign from in front of the stool next to the wall where he could push his back to the wall. He took his usual post, and Dem settled onto the stool beside him. His knees pushed against Dem's hip and thigh.

"Joker, want your usual," Twitch asked.

Twitch was small and feminine, he had this energy that was infectious. Twitch always wanted everyone around him happy. It must've been a busy night already because Twitch had his long black hair twisted up into a messy bun.

"What can I get for your friend?" Twitch attempted to hide his curiosity but failed.

The boy was nosy as fuck, and he was also a matchmaker. Shit, he made himself a target, just what he didn't need.

"Hi, Twitch, I'm Dem, could I just get a water please?"

"Sure thing, Dem."

This wasn't the place for intimate conversation, the music too loud, and a tension of unleashed violence thick in the packed room.

Dem turned to him and leaned in, he stood his ground and didn't flinch away. Warm breath fanned his jaw, then his ear.

38

"Just because you brought me to a bar doesn't mean we can't talk. It only makes it where we have to get closer. Don't think I'm not onto you, Jackson."

"Shit."

His muttered curse earned him a chuckle from Dem. The man straightened as their drinks arrived.

"You're so cute together," Twitch squealed and did a little hip wiggle.

"We're not—"

"Thank you, Twitch. Has he always been so stubborn?"

"You have no idea, he's a nightmare, but some great and plentiful sex should loosen him up a bit," Twitch said and winked. "Okay, back to work, holler when you need a refill."

"I like him."

"He's married."

"Yeah, I know that, and he's not my type, Jackson."

"I gotta take a piss," he announced and surged off the bar stool. He headed for the hallway that led to the bathrooms.

He needed a minute to himself, the close-quarter conversation hadn't been in the plan. The music and all was supposed to make talking impossible, but he should've known better. Hadn't he watched his friends over the years, the way they'd get close, whisper in each other's ears, and exchange kisses between sentences, sometimes words?

He ducked into the women's room knowing it would be empty and leaned his back against the door. The music muffled on the other side.

"Why are you hiding in the women's room?"

His eyes flew open, and he found a grinning Hunter seated on the bathroom sink. Hunter was married to Wren and also Linus. How did they keep each other happy? How weren't they jealous? Something in his gut told him if he had a man of his own that he'd be jealous—possessive of the man he considered his.

"Why are you?"

"I come in here for my breaks, Twitch does too, but normally he isn't alone."

"I fucked up, man."

"And how is that? Start a brawl already? I've only been in here ten minutes, so you couldn't have done too much damage."

"No, I brought a guy here."

"Please tell me this isn't the first fucking date, Joker?" Hunter waved his hands in the air. "Don't even answer that, it is. You know a first date should be in a restaurant, where y'all can talk and get to know each other."

"This was supposed to scare him off so he'd give up on this dating me thing."

Hunter threw his back and laughed his ass off at him.

"What the fuck is so funny?"

"You, Joker, come on, the man wants to date *you* after meeting you and your charming personality. Wren said he threatened you not to kill Dem."

"How did you know it was Dem?"

"Everyone else in town knows you and are mostly frightened of you, it had to be a newbie."

"But why me? Fuck, I hate this shit."

"You just hate people liking you, even though your friends love your cranky ass."

"I don't know how to do this, you know—"

"I don't know shit, Joker. I know you, you're fiercely protective, like you are with Harper. I know most of the shit you get into is when some asshole thinks he can put

40

his hands on a woman or someone weaker than them, different than them. You might not think so, but you're a pretty great guy when you're not trying to kill someone."

"All this mushy talk is making me want to puke."

"Then get back to your date. If what I hear is right, he's pretty fucking hot. He's probably got a ring around him at the bar right now."

"Fuck." He stormed out of the bathroom and down the hall. He hated when other people were right. It wasn't a ring, but it was enough.

Some pretty boy in leathers was all up on Dem. The man's hand on Dem's lower back. He could almost hear the sweet talking going on. Maybe he should let it, Dem could go home—fuck no. He squared his shoulders and stretched to his full height of six-three. He wasn't the most muscular man around, but it didn't always take a bodybuilder frame to take a fucker down.

He walked over, stopped behind Dem, and took the stranger's wrist in a steely grip.

"He gave you permission to touch him?"

"Jackson, I was just telling this gentleman my date would be right back." Dem turned to him.

He didn't take his glare off the pretty boy. He made himself not tense up when Dem's arm went around his waist. He released the guy fast enough for the stranger to stumble a bit. Soft fingertips touched his jaw and turned his head to look at Dem. Dem was smiling at him, his long, wavy hair framed his face. He didn't like the way that smile made him feel. He didn't like any of it. It made him feel off; like he wasn't himself.

"Jackson, don't kill him."

Then it happened, lips that were soft beyond belief touched his. He heard a pain-filled grunt, but he was too focused on his first kiss. A steel-band circled his chest. He jerked away.

"We have to go."

"Okay."

Pity didn't exist in the depths of Dem's eyes. Dem's lush mouth still curved into a content, almost sweet smile. He needed to get away—now.

6 This Was Suicide

"Why did I let you all talk me into this," Dem yelled over the roar of a Cessna's engine. He stared at Sin and Saint, backup singers and drummers for Executioners. The maniacal expressions on their too pretty faces came close to eclipsing the fear of jumping from a perfectly good fucking plane.

Jackson had been gone two weeks without a word. He'd searched everywhere until he came across the twins a week ago and they said they knew where to find him. The last week was spent practicing skydiving under the tutelage of the world's craziest ex-male models turned sex shop managers, and they deemed him ready. What the fuck was he thinking?

"Bitch, this is romantic as fuck. You're so getting laid after this one." Sin grinned maniacally as he checked the shoot release. "We've done this jump plenty of times. Just do what we taught you. We know just when to jump to land in Joker's clearing. You got this. If you're lucky, they'll be spankings involved."

He'd never been spanked in his life, but, maybe it held merit, especially if it was Jackson doing it. He hadn't planned the kiss at Brawlers. How could he not though when Jackson looked so jealous and possessive of another man touching him? He didn't typically find jealousy an attractive quality so getting turned on by Jackson's actions made him a bit crazy. He'd kissed Jackson, and the man tensed. Why he sensed it was Jackson's first kiss, he didn't know.

He wondered how many firsts he could have of Jackson's.

"Down, boy, until you get to your man. As impressive as that is, we're holding on for one man in particular."

Sin and Saint had a thing for Sheriff Camden Pelter, and they made no secret of it. It became a huge joke around town. He felt sorry for Camden when the man stopped running.

"Two minutes to drop zone," Saint hollered.

"I can't do this."

"You can, Dem. You've jumped tandem with us several times. This is no different. Your legs won't be able to hold you, though, so make sure you hold them up the best you can...go into a slide. You got this. We'll bring the chopper out in a few days to lift you out."

"What if I'm dead by then?"

"We'll circle until you wave us off."

"I wasn't talking about the fall killing me."

"Joker is a sweetheart, he just likes to play tough. You have supplies for a few days. I threw in lube and condoms. I know he doesn't have them."

"Sixty seconds until drop."

His arm crutches were strapped to a small pack of supplies that would be dropped after he jumped. He breathed deeply through his nose and out through his mouth as he crossed his arms over his chest, with Sin holding onto the straps of his parachute.

"Ten, nine, eight…"

He closed his eyes as Sin and Saint counted down, at one he let himself fall back, and he spun in the air. His eyes flew open as the wind whipped as his skin. Adrenaline pumped through his system as an overwhelming sense of freedom took over. The landscape below looked so different, trees and bushes indistinguishable. A tiny blob he knew was Jackson's hideout set in the middle of a large clearing. He mentally counted down, reached up and pulled the lever, the force of the chute opening jarred him. He steered himself just like Sin and Saint told him to do.

As the ground drew closer, he forced himself to brace as his legs collided with the ground, then he slid along the cushion of grass. He laid there as the parachute collapsed around him. A huge smile pulled at the corners of his mouth. He'd just jumped from an airplane for the first time in his life without Sin or Saint behind him. Laughter filled his ears, and he realized he was lying on the ground giggling.

"What the fuck, Sin, Saint, what are you—"

The fabric disappeared, and he was staring up at Jackson. Jackson's shocked expression alone was worth it.

"Dem, are you crazy? Are you okay? I'm going to kill them for this," Jackson bellowed and cursed.

Strong hands searched every inch of his arms, legs, torso, his neck, oh yes, his neck. He loved his neck—

"Are you okay? You're not…give me your goddamned phone so I can get you help."

"I'm fine, that was fucking amazing! Did you see me? I jumped, and I lived."

"Maybe, but I might kill you and then those little shit friends of yours."

The *Cessna* flew low over the tree line, making wide circles until he waved his arms. The plane pitched left and right in the signal they devised to tell him to have fun.

"I don't know how to repack my chute."

"We'll just roll it up. What the fuck were you thinking?"

"You ran from me."

"I didn't run, I come out here to think. They know not to fuck with me. They fly over, I give them proof of life, and they leave me the fuck alone."

"Now you're stuck with me for two days. What you gonna do with me?"

"Hide your body?"

He sighed. "You're so romantic."

"Get up, so we can get you out of that pack and suit."

Oh, that was worth it. Jackson's arms were around him and lifted him from the ground, helping to his feet. He felt the tugs to his side, and then he rested his weight against Jackson's hard, muscular frame. He pressed his face into the curve of Jackson's neck as the weight of the pack disappeared. The thigh straps slid down his leg, and he faintly listened to the soft thud of the rig falling to the ground. He wasn't paying attention, Jackson smelled like sweat, wood smoke, and something spicy and manly.

"Can you walk or do you need me to carry you?"

"You'd carry me?"

"If you—"

"No, no, I'm fine, I can make it. They were sending down a pack with my crutches and supplies."

"Can you stand for a minute or do you need to sit down?"

"Probably need to sit down until you find the pack."

"Won't be too hard, it's rainbow like your chute."

Jackson helped him sit back down, and he watched as Jackson headed off toward the tree line. Just like Jackson said, a hiking pack dangled from a tree by a chute tangled on limbs. Jackson grabbed the pack with a few days of clothes, supplies, and the extras Sin and Saint threw in and strode back to him. Jackson removed his crutches and handed them to him.

Once he got to his feet, he straightened and took the back pack, hoisting the strap onto his shoulder. He slipped his forearms into his crutches. Backing up a few steps he observed Jackson rolling everything up and tucked it under his arm.

If it was possible for steam to come out of a man's ears, Jackson's would. Was it insane that he was trapped in the middle of nowhere with a man with tentative control of his anger and completely ecstatic about it? Probably was but he didn't care. He said the same to Gideon, Harper, and the rest of the crews when they told him he should just leave Jackson alone. They'd left him alone far too much in his opinion. Those days were over, and Jackson better get used to it.

"You look exceptionally handsome today, Jackson."

"I'm not happy with you right now."

He bit the inside of his cheek to keep from laughing. That became almost impossible when he noticed Killer giving him a Jackson death glare from her perch on a camp chair. She had a black mini-skull and crossbones hoodie and a spiked collar. How they found Jackson a dog with the man's exact personality astounded him.

Jackson tossed the bundle next to the open door. Smoke came from a metal chimney.

"Would I be safe in assuming we're roughing it for the next two days?"

"No electricity. No indoor plumbing. There's a hot spring for baths. Welcome to nature, city boy."

He hadn't gone camping in forever, but his Da was a big believer in tents and camp showers. Nothing Jackson would put him through was strange to him. He'd grown up on a ranch in Wyoming before he'd struck out for culinary school.

"Somewhere I can put my bag?"

Jackson held out his hand with a huff.

He smiled sweetly and handed over the pack. The man took it, and he batted his lashes as he watched Jackson. Anger highlighted Jackson's cheeks.

The man was just too hot for his own good. Jackson disappeared into the shack and returned a few minutes later with two sandwiches and bottles of water. Jackson ordered Killer off the chair. The micro snarl warned of later retribution. He wondered if he had to sleep with one eye open as Jackson pointed him toward the chair.

He barely settled in when the man laid a sandwich and bottle on his lap. Jackson sat down on the ground next to a small fire. The man ate silently, with small bites, and chewed slowly. He'd listened to Harper outline Jackson's diet, he had known about the pancakes, but one sandwich and a single bottle of water wasn't enough for a man Jackson's size.

Jackson wasn't an overly muscular man, not bulky and not skinny either. The muscles of his arms were lean. He noticed something he'd never seen before. Jackson wore a short-sleeved t-shirt. Long, raised scars curved around his upper arms, the skin of his wrists bore thick, uneven grooves. He moved his attention to Jackson's hands, a few fingers were crooked, and his nails were abnormally short and pitted.

He frowned at the thoughts that entered his head. Images fed by the snippets of Jackson's behavior he'd learned from his friends, things he'd noticed, and Jackson's aversion to touch.

"You're not eating," Jackson stated without looking at him.

"You can have it, I'm not hungry."

"You should eat."

That's when Jackson turned to look at him. The man stopped eating his own lunch.

"Eat."

That one word broached no argument.

He nodded and lifted the sandwich, taking a small bite. Plain peanut butter. The bread was slightly stale. He really wasn't hungry, and his chaotic thoughts weren't helping. His mind tried to figure out who had hurt Jackson. Who had caused the man to shy away from the most basic of affection?

Guilt assailed him as he realized what he'd done. All he'd wanted was to get to Jackson. Spend time alone and get to know him. But did he ruin Jackson's sanctuary? He felt like a selfish asshole, maybe he should've listened when they said to leave Jackson's alone.

"Don't look at them."

"Look at what?"

"People think I'm crazy, and they're right. But I'm not stupid."

"I didn't think you were, Jackson, and I don't think you're crazy either."

Jackson snorted and went back to eating.

He finished off the sandwich so as not to offend Jackson.

"Why do you come out here?"

"It's quiet."

"It's beautiful too. How did you find this place?"

"My grandfather owned the land. When I got out of prison, I came out here and built the shack. Lived out here for few years."

"Is he still alive?"

"Drank himself to death a year after I got out. You're not asking what I did?"

"I'm curious, I won't lie about that, but you'll tell me if you want."

"When I was sixteen, I beat my old man to death." Jackson surged to his feet. "I gotta go get more firewood."

He didn't try to call Jackson back. The man needed time, and so did he. He hadn't expected Jackson to answer him, and he didn't know how he felt about the one he got.

The scars made sense but what did they mean? What had Jackson's father done to him and how much damage had the man caused?

7 What Was He Supposed to do With Dem?

He crouched down and stacked the last load of firewood next to the potbellied stove. It was more than he needed, but he had to keep Dem warm through the night. He didn't understand why he cared. The only person he'd given much thought to was Harper. She was his best friend and put up with him, even when he didn't understand why she did.

It was dark outside, and he'd kept the small fire going in the pit. Dem remained strangely quiet. Well, he did announce that he'd killed his old man like he would say it was raining outside. Probably not what a man wanted to hear when he was trapped in the middle of nowhere with a killer.

He plopped down onto his ass and stared into the dancing flames inside the stove.

He glanced over his shoulder when Dem cleared his throat.

"You want me to handle dinner? It's been awhile since I cooked over a camp fire, but I think I remember how."

"All I brought was—"

"I got you covered, I know what my man likes," Dem said with a wink and picked up the bag beside the door.

Dem turned away before he had a chance to say anything. He just watched Dem through the door, the man dug into the pack. He was curious, but he couldn't make himself move. When he saw the rainbow parachute making its way to the ground, all he'd thought about was taking Sin or Saint out for being stupid. They knew better than to bother him. Instead of them, he found Dem on the ground.

He'd had a moment of fear before it changed to anger. He'd hiked in more than three miles. He kept the place overgrown to keep others out.

Then it hit him, Dem had parachuted in to spend time with him. Why would someone like Dem even bother?

"Jackson, do you have some cast iron pans around here?"

"Yeah, just hold on."

He went to an old metal locker sitting in the corner of the structure. He pulled open the door, getting the grate and pan, also tugged out the extra sleeping bag he kept there for winter.

Taking deep, even breaths, he calmed himself and made his way outside. Two steaks that still looked partially frozen laid on some aluminum foil.

"The freezer bag worked really well. Dinner might take a bit longer than I expected."

He took a seat in the camp chair and set the requested items beside Dem who knelt beside the fire. Dem had his long, wavy hair tucked behind his ears.

"You didn't have to go to the trouble."

"Just like you didn't have to go to the trouble of modifying your bike to take me out."

"It was no big deal."

"Yes, it was. I don't think anyone else would've done it. Especially when I know you didn't really want to go out with me. Is it because of my…if you're not attracted to me because of the crutches I can take it, you know?"

"Don't be an idiot."

"Thanks."

"Fuck, that's…I'm broken and damaged goods. I'm not worth the effort."

"I don't think that at all."

Dem spoke without looking at him.

"My friends know not to come out here."

"I got all the warnings. Sin and Saint were just crazy enough not to care and thought it was so romantic."

He snorted. "They would."

"I can call them in the morning to airlift me out."

"You're here, and I was planning on leaving in a few days anyway. I got jobs waiting."

"Why did you kill him?"

He wanted to scare him off, and the story he had to tell was gruesome enough to do that.

"My mother was thirteen when my…Garnet cornered her on her way home from school. He bent her over the seat of his truck and raped her, took her back to his cabin, did it again and again. I found her journals when I was twelve, and I read them all. Every last word of what he'd done to her for nine years. It was her rage, the only way she could get it out. The fucker dropped her off like it was a fucking date…like he hadn't left her with physical scars inside and out."

"Jackson, you—"

"You wanted to know. She disappeared after my eighth birthday. They said she just left, but he killed her, I know he did. I wished she was still alive, maybe found happiness elsewhere."

"She loved you, I'm sure she wouldn't have left you willingly."

"She probably didn't. I still hope she's alive, but thirty years is a long time to stay away."

"Did he do that to you?"

He noticed Dem pointed toward the deep grooved scars around his wrists…there were more. There wasn't much of his body that didn't bear the marks.

"He tied my wrists down when he smashed my fingertips or removed my nails." He looked down at his hands, they had more scars from working as a mechanic, but the worst were the ones Garnet gave him. "I got so used to the pain, that he needed to up the stakes. I could take it, I was a professional at surviving the torture. He wanted to make me a man just like him.

"I knew about the abuse, I wasn't stupid. I knew he took out his anger on my mom, but when I read what he'd done…all the pain she survived. He came home one night, drunk and started his usual bullshit. Instead of taking it, I started hitting, and I didn't stop. I was told the Sheriff found me wandering covered in blood. Garnet's face was destroyed. They charged me, I was in prison until my twenty—"

He flinched as he had a lap full of man. Full lips pressed tender kisses to his face. His eyes closed and there was a gentle brush to his lashes, then to his cheeks. Then Dem's mouth hovered against his. The lush curves trembled against his thinner lips.

"You don't want to do this," Joker said, but even as he did, he raised his hand, his fingertips barely skimmed Dem's cheek. The wetness under his touch had his eyes opening.

"You want to hear something stalkerish?"

The question was odd after what he confessed, but he was curious, and hopefully it would be a distraction. He nodded.

"I thought you were beautiful the first time I saw your picture on Gideon and Harper's mantle. I even pulled it down when I'd get home from work and look at it."

"That's creepy."

"Shut up, it's romantic."

"Whatever you say."

"So, I'm going to kiss you, and you're going to let me."

"I am?"

Dem made a sound he took as an affirmative, and then Dem pressed their mouths together.

A moment of panic tightened his chest, he started to pull away, but strong hands curved around the back of his head. He understood pain, could protect himself against it. This was something else, he held still…and waited.

"This works better when you participate, baby."

Dem whispered against his mouth.

"No one touches me."

"Too damn bad, I want to touch you and often."

"Why?"

"Because you're worth it."

It was all Dem said before the kisses started again. Just gentle nips at his lips. Just once he wanted to know what his friends had, that was all, so he followed Dem's lead. He sucked at the softness of Dem's bottom lip, and it earned him a moan. Something about that sound urged him on, he wanted more of them. Those deep groans, sweet and needy, and he increased the pressure. His kisses turned rougher, more dominant, and he combed his fingers through Dem's soft hair. He tugged, and Dem gasped. He dipped his tongue passed Dem's parted lips.

His cock hardened and jerked, pushed into Dem's hip. Dem whimpered and shook on his lap, he must be doing something right to have Dem react the way he was. Then a tiny rumbling body pushed between them.

"Killer, me and you are going to have problems. He's mine too."

"Who says I'm yours?"

"I do," Dem said and kissed him again. "I'm going to finish making dinner. That monster down your thigh is a bit…yeah, not talking about cock, nope," Dem mumbled to himself as Dem slid off his lap.

He rubbed Killer's head as she burrowed under his shirt, it was her favorite place when he didn't have his hoodie on. She curled into a ball on his stomach and huffed loudly.

"She's going to have to learn to share."

"Just because we kissed you don't get—"

"You're mine, I'll give you time to get used to it."

Dem seemed to ignore him after that statement, and he watched Dem focus on cooking steaks, cutting up potatoes, then everything started sizzling in the pan. He looked down at the still thick bulge in his jeans and tried to remember the last time he got a hard-on. He despised touching himself. His jerk off sessions were quick and pointless, he never got off. The few times he had, once he'd felt the scars under his hand, his dick went limp.

The man hadn't seen him yet. Not the patchwork landscape of his body, the deep grooves from whip and blade. Most had gotten infected and hadn't healed the way they should've. A secret part of him craved pleasure, someone soft and gentle, someone who wanted to make him feel good rather than suffer. Could he even do it?

He'd allowed Dem to sit on his lap and didn't push him away. He'd allowed the man to kiss him. But could he be normal? He couldn't see passed his rage most days. Existing in a chaotic vortex that pushed him to fight—to hurt. Dem would give up when he learned just how broken and sick he was. No matter how much he wanted to experience pleasure, there was something about the pain— the familiarity of it. He been born of violence, destined for it, and he was trapped. The man would run. He just needed to wait him out.

8 Damn, Dem was Cold

The thick padding of the sleeping bag did nothing to keep out the night chill. He didn't expect the south to get that cold, but there he was shivering. He tossed onto his back then his side to watch Jackson sleep. Last night he'd done the same thing. His man had his sleeping bag as far from his as the walls of the shack allowed. He wasn't hurt by it...much. The kisses they'd shared were more than he'd expected. He savored the memory even as he craved more.

His face flushed as he remembered the minute Jackson had lost a bit of control. Jackson strong fingers had fisted in his hair and tugged. He'd never really thought about someone being rough with him. No one was ever anything but gentle with him. Over the years, he'd quickly grown tired of the lovers he'd had. The *are you alright* questions. Even in the middle of sex, he was made to feel different—less than.

He slammed his eyes closed and tucked deeper into the bag.

"Are you going to sleep anytime soon?"

"I'm sorry, I'm cold." He hated that it sounded like he was whining, but he was.

There was a deep, sexy growl from Jackson, then the man was on his feet and headed his way. He let out an unmanly squeak as he was manhandled, flipped this way and that. He hugged himself when the sleeping bag was unzipped, and he watched as Jackson fastened their bags together. His head rested on Jackson's bicep, then Killer was suddenly pushing under into the bag and curled up against his stomach.

"Sleep."

"How the hell am I supposed to sleep?"

"Close your eyes and sleep."

He sensed Jackson tense more than felt it when he tucked his head under Jackson's bearded chin. A beard and mustache that were thicker than they were two weeks ago. He liked the burly facial hair but had a feeling Jackson would trim it as soon as he got home.

"You're not going to sleep, are you?"

"No, I want to ask you a question."

"I won't guarantee I'll answer."

"Do you think I'm weak?"

"No, why would...you're fine."

"Other men I've dated..." He smiled at Joker's possessive grumble. "They treated me different."

"Then they're assholes, got nothing to do with you."

"I want to touch you."

"You are."

"No, like..." He slid his left hand under Jackson's hoodie and t-shirt.

"Don't."

"Please?"

Jackson remained stiff, but he didn't push him away, progress.

He touched the flat plane of Jackson's stomach, felt the dips and ridges of scar tissue. His eyes burned, but he suppressed the tears. He couldn't even imagine the pain Jackson went through. He didn't care what Jackson thought, he wasn't disgusted by the scars, only by what caused them. Some of the marks felt bumpy, others were silky smooth, and he was curious what they would feel like under his lips and tongue. Turn the memory of pain into pleasure, but he knew Jackson wouldn't allow it—yet.

"Did you ever try to find her?"

"If she wanted to be found she would've contacted me. Why would she want to look at me? I look like him."

"I'm sure she loved you."

"If she ain't dead, then she's somewhere happy. It's all I care about."

He let it go, but maybe he could talk to Linus. It wasn't like Jackson had to know. Thirty years is a long time to stay hidden, maybe it was best that she did, but he needed to try. Maybe it would take away some of Jackson's bad memories.

He rested his hand over Jackson's heart and closed his eyes. He didn't want to push his luck with Jackson too much.

"Dammit, I'll carry you out."

He grinned at Jackson as the man mumbled curses under his breath. Jackson had made Sin and Saint land the helicopter instead of the twins staying at a safe distance and lifting him out with a safety harness.

"I'll be fine, the twins are certified and everything."

"Of course they're certifiable."

"That's not what I meant."

"What happens if they—"

He pushed a quick kiss to Jackson's mouth, and he laughed at the drawn out aw's behind him, but he didn't miss the momentary gasps beforehand.

"Dem got the D, wait until—"

"Saint, if you want to live, which is questionable after dropping him out here, then I wouldn't finish."

"Come on, Joker," Saint whined.

Even as twins and nearly identical, you could tell them apart, especially their voices. Sin had a huskier tone than Saint, who's voice was quiet and sweet.

"No, this shit goes nowhere else."

"So, you got the D instead of—"

Jackson lunged for Sin, and he barely held Jackson back. He felt if Jackson wanted to get passed him, the man would.

"Quit, you know he's busting your balls on purpose. I'll be fine. I'll be home before you even pack up and hike out. You're staying a few extra days?"

"How—"

"You need time. Can I sleep at your place until you come home?"

He knew he'd interrupted Jackson's thinking time, and he wouldn't begrudge Jackson a few more days to himself. That didn't mean he didn't want to be in Jackson's space. It was also a huge risk on Jackson's part. The man was obsessive about his space and things. He wondered how little Jackson had of his own over the years. The time with an abusive parent, in prison, and he wanted to be Jackson's, yet knew it wouldn't be as easy as saying so.

"Why would you want to do that?"

"Say yes, Jackson, and give me a damn key."

Jackson was so cute when he growled and glared, he wondered if there was some bite with that growl. Okay, so not the time for that.

"It's never locked, no one fucks with me."

He pointed at Joker. "Behave and be careful."

"Behave?"

"Yeah, don't be picking up single, hot hikers on your way home."

Jackson rolled his eyes and shook his head.

"Shut up and go."

"Yes, dear."

Sin and Saint rushed forward, grabbing his bag and the wrapped parachute. The twins avoided getting anywhere near Jackson, but he couldn't miss the mischievous little smiles that curved their glossed lips. Jackson stepped back, and he suddenly didn't want to leave. Just because everything in him screamed Jackson was his that didn't mean the man was ready to give in.

As Sin helped him into the chopper, the young man leaned in.

"He yours yet?"

"He was always mine, he just needs to admit it."

Sin and Saint just grinned.

He secured himself onto the bench seat and tucked his crutches between his thighs. He peeked out the still open door and watched Jackson stare at them as they took off. Killer's tiny frame leaned against Joker's ankle. It was almost painful to leave. He'd spent two days in Jackson's company—just the two of them. There were cuddles and kisses, and Jackson told him things he was sure Jackson never told anyone.

In his gut, he knew Jackson only did it trying to scare him away, but Jackson didn't know him well enough yet. He was his mother's son, like she got her man, he was determined to get Jackson.

"You really staying at Joker's place?"

"Yes, I am. But I need to go home and pack a bag first."

"Wow, you do know Joker is possessive of his things? We heard the rumors about his old man. It's said Joker had a bare mattress on the floor and nothing else. Kept him chained—"

"Jackson will tell me all that when he wants. It's not my business."

It was completely his business, but he didn't want to give away Jackson's secrets, no matter how close the reality was to rumor. He wanted the stories from Jackson himself—given freely.

He also had plans, and he needed Jackson gone for a few days. It might get him a spanking which he was looking forward to, but he was going to do it anyway. He'd listened to every story their mutual friends shared about Jackson, got a feel for his likes and dislikes. So, they were going to work on Jackson's boundaries and knocking those fuckers down.

He smiled at the plans forming, the thoughts of sleeping in Jackson's bed, and knowing that Jackson was allowing him into his private space. He was going to make sure Jackson didn't regret it. Coming there might have been temporary, but no longer. This was home, and he was going to settle in, whether Jackson like it or not.

9 Peaches Needed to Stop Busting his Balls

"Please, for everything unholy in the world would you put on some fucking clothes," Joker growled as he looked everywhere but at his naked lawyer. In the end, he focused on her bare toes, that seemed safe enough. He wrung his hands in the pocket of his sweatshirt and disturbed a sleeping Killer which earned him a menacing growl.

His dog was a little pissed at him for using her a little too much as his security blanket the last month. He knew she needed her space even if she still stayed curled up in his hoodie to be near him.

"Shouldn't have come to my place at midnight. Besides this is a nudist friendly house. What the hell do you want?"

"I didn't want to go home...there's someone there."

Peaches gasped and spun, he glanced up and realized his mistake as he slapped his hands over his eyes. The woman laughed her head off at him.

"Why is there someone in your trailer? Are there things you're not telling me?"

He removed his hands from his eyes, but to be on the safe side, he kept them closed. He loved the woman, he did, he just couldn't take seeing her naked again. It would be like seeing his mother naked. It wasn't right.

"Ghost's friend, Dem."

Okay, he wasn't positive Dem was still at his place. But what he knew of Dem, he could almost be sure that the man wouldn't let him get away easily. He didn't understand, he was a bastard, he wasn't even that attractive and to be honest, even if he was, the amount of scar tissue covering his body would deter any normal person.

"Sexy fucker that Demetri. He likes you?"

"You don't have to sound so shocked by it."

The defensiveness took him by surprise. Wasn't he just admitting to himself he was shocked by Dem wanting anything to do with him?

"I am. If you fill me in, I'll even put on a robe?"

"I'll confess to crimes I never committed."

"Joker, I'm your lawyer, I know all your crimes."

He listened to her bare feet shuffle on the carpet as she disappeared and returned a few minutes later.

"So, tell me."

He turned his head to look at her and heavily exhaled as he tried to get his thoughts together. He proceeded to fill her in on everything from the smiley face pancakes to Dem parachuting onto his property.

"Oh fake zombie Jesus, that's so romantic."

"Why are all y'all saying how romantic it is? There's gotta be something wrong with the man. I told him I beat my old man to death."

"Justifiable homicide, Joker. I worked my ass off to get your sentence commuted to time served. I'm just sorry I couldn't get it completely expunged."

"You did what you could. I could still be locked up."

He sighed as he watched her sit down on the opposite end of the couch.

"Joker, you're not seventeen anymore being locked up with grown men. You sure as hell ain't the same twenty-one-year-old that walked out of prison. Why won't you give some man a chance?"

"I'm damaged—"

"Bullshit, Joker. I've dealt with damaged, I've defended every kind of criminal from small time petty shit to gangsters. Most of them had a reason for doing what they did. Ain't my place to judge. Garnet was fucked up from the time he was born. Your grandfather kept him locked up out in the woods. No schooling. Didn't teach that boy any morals and what did Garnet do? Did the same thing his father did and his father before him. Keeping yourself locked up in your trailer, with your strict routine and punishing yourself isn't breaking the cycle, honey."

"What if I'm just like them?"

"You're not."

"What if I am? What if—"

"You're going to kill yourself with the what ifs in life. What if Mary was five minutes later or earlier, and Garnet missed her completely. That isn't what happened. Garnet did horrendous things to your mother. I read the journals, introduced them as evidence at your re-sentencing hearing.

What Garnet did to you was monstrous, and he got what he deserved."

No matter how many times someone told him it was justified, he still remembered all the times he'd fantasized about killing Garnet. Slow and as painful as every act Garnet had done to him. It didn't change the fact that he lived for rage and violence—he didn't know any other way to exist.

"You're thinking too hard. You've lived the life of a monk, honey, denying yourself the basic need of every human—touch. And I'm not talking fucking, anyone can have sex, I'm talking intimacy."

"I don't know how to do all that shit."

"That's because no one ever taught you how. Okay, Lawyer/Client confidentiality begins now, whatever we say goes nowhere, not even Gib."

He snorted. "You tell Gib everything."

"Not what happens between me and clients, so, talk to me, ask whatever it is you want to know."

"I'm not asking my lawyer for a fucking birds and bees lesson."

"I think it would technically be a bees and bees lesson."

"Quit busting my balls."

"Well, some people actually like that sort of shit."

"I hate you."

"No, you don't, you love me, Joker."

"I can't...you know."

"Oh, that's a common problem with men of your age. Well, my Gib never had the issue, man can still pound—"

"No! There is nothing wrong with my dick. Fake Zombie Jesus, are you stoned?"

"No, me and Lily didn't meet up tonight like normal."

"Isn't there some kind of law against stoner lawyers?"

"I'm not that kind of lawyer. So, what *is* the issue if it's not keeping it up for your man?"

Joker should've gone home to his trailer. Dem would've been less trouble than dealing with Peaches. He groaned and dropped his head back onto the couch, staring up at the ceiling. Soft, gentle fingers combed through his hair, nails soothingly scratched his scalp.

"I can't get passed what Garnet did."

"You're probably never going to. We can ignore most of the emotional and mental scars we're left with, but you have physical scars, marks that can never be healed or washed away. Do you think Demetri will be disgusted?"

"He's touched—"

"Touched, oh, oh, why didn't you lead with the *he touched me* portion of this painful Q and A?"

"I don't see how Gib hasn't divorced you yet."

"Don't be mean."

"That's exactly it, I'm mean and violent."

"What happened the last time I had to come spring you from jail?"

"That fucker from the feed store grabbed his wife's arm. She flinched, and I saw other bruises."

"You're like the Powers' Vigilante. You see someone put their hands on their significant other or their children and you act. You hear a rumor, and you make a visit to warn them you better not hear another one. You're nothing like Garnet. Is Crave like his old man, would he ever—"

"I'd kill him first." Crave kept himself away from Twitch for years because he feared he'd be just like his old man, but Crave was different. Crave was insane in a good way. He didn't have that luxury.

"He dotes on that husband of his. Twitch can't get enough of Crave. You know what you're going to do?"

"What?" He was almost terrified to ask. He's known Peaches for over twenty years. She'd stayed by his side through his worst. Took his case when his other public defender dropped the ball and let sixteen-year-old him be sentenced as an adult. Never once had that bastard introduced his medical records—years of abuse and torture.

"You're going to get your ass up and go home to your man."

"Not my—"

"A man who has done all the things you mentioned for you, that is a man who if he isn't yours, he wants to be."

"What if—"

"Knock off the what ifs, Joker, we get limited time on this planet. There's nothing after this. We have this one sometimes shit-stained life, and there's no time for the regrets of what could've been. Love as hard or harder than the rage you think eats away at you. Replace that anger with passion and let yourself love and be loved on."

He remained silent as he rolled his head and looked at the maternal look on Peaches' face.

"And, Joker, there's something you're forgetting, or it may never have occurred to you."

"I'm scared."

She chuckled and leaned in to kiss his cheek.

"You need control, a comfort zone, why not play a little game with your man? Mental foreplay is sometimes more erotic than touch. It can be a little sexting, maybe a dirty midnight phone call, or better yet—"

"I couldn't—"

"Go home, ask your man to strip and tell him exactly what you want him to do for you. A little voyeurism can keep things interesting, and you can see how your man touches himself, what he likes before you ever have to lay—"

"I'm out." He surged from the couch with the crazy woman cackling behind him.

"Joker, please, just think about it. You need to ease into the touching and what better way to learn about your partner than knowing what he likes. Maybe he doesn't want a gentleman or someone who's had the world handed to him—maybe he just wants you. I love you, Jackson, as much as I love Landon and the rest of my adopted children. You're as much a part of my heart as any of them. Remember that, and don't ever forget, I didn't give birth to you, but I've considered you mine for over twenty years."

"Th—thanks, Peaches."

"Anytime. Now, go home and see Demetri."

He nodded and bent to give her a quick hug, then pulled away and rushed for the door. It was easier to let Peaches, Lily, or Harper touch him, even if he kept the contact brief it was still hard for him to accept or give affection. With men, it was damn near impossible. He was shocked by how easily he'd let Dem touch, kiss him, and sit on his lap.

He hopped into his run-down pickup, started the engine and took off toward home. Killer huffed in his pocket. He was killing her routine and his.

It wasn't a long drive, and he slightly regretted the briefness of it. He pulled in the driveway beside the shop and saw his trailer. The windows were dark. He wondered if Dem had even come there. No sign of a strange vehicle. He turned off his truck and got out, he slammed the door.

He pulled the latch, it wasn't locked, and pulled it open, ascending the three metal steps. He dragged Killer out and bent to set her on the floor. She instantly ran to the one small bedroom. The street lights illuminated a naked man in the middle of his bed. Dem's pale, rounded ass exposed. The sheet bunched around Dem's bare thighs. Dem was laid on his stomach, but with his left leg bent to the side. Killer took the steps he'd built at the end of the bed for her. She barely paid attention to Dem as she curled up against the man's side after she made several circles to get comfortable. He ducked into the tiny bathroom and stripped off quickly, then stepped into the cramped shower stall.

He efficiently washed, not lingering anywhere. The quicker he cleaned, the more he was able to ignore the scars under his hands. He stepped out and dried his body roughly. Stepping out into the dark main room, he was thankful for the darkness and the fact he didn't see Dem wake up when Killer laid down beside him.

When he entered his room, he turned to the left to open one of the built-in drawers.

"Don't."

He jerked his gaze to find Dem's eyes open, illuminated by the outside light.

"Lay down with me. Nothing between us."

"I don't think that's a good idea."

"Probably not, but please, just once."

He took a deep breath and let it out roughly. Turning, he put his right knee onto the bed and laid down behind Dem. He shivered at the soft, smooth skin pressed fully to his hairier body. He hadn't thought about manscaping before in his life, but wondered if—

"Fuck, you feel good," Dem whispered.

There was an odd tone in his voice. He'd heard it before from the people he called friends. It was reverence—need. Dem didn't try to turn toward him, simply lifted Killer and pulled the sheet over them, then placed Killer on top.

His dog didn't even move.

He laid his arm over Dem, and the man sighed and scooting closer to him. He held still as he waited for the fear. The accustomed rage to rip through him. He didn't know how to feel when neither emotion came. He couldn't remember a time he'd slept with anyone. He knew everyone assumed the truth about him, although, no one dared say it out loud.

His old man, his grandfather, they hadn't understood the word no, the same thing that happened to his mother happened to his grandmother too. She'd committed suicide. There hadn't been another way to happiness for her. No other escape. She'd ran away so many times, and his grandfather always dragged her back. His childhood had been filled with nightmares. Even if there was a small sliver of a chance that he was like them, he wouldn't give in.

"Relax and quit thinking so hard, just go to sleep."

Dem relaxed, and he tried to follow suit, he had to be up in four hours to start his day. He wasn't a selfish man, and he didn't require much in life, but tonight he wanted to be selfish. To understand what his friends always talked about. Dem couldn't be his, but one moment of selfishness of his thirty-eight years couldn't hurt, right?

10 Dem Was Looking Forward to a Spanking

Five, four, three, two…

He counted down and didn't even get to one before he heard Jackson's gruff bellow through the order window.

"What the fuck is this shit, I didn't—"

"Watch your mouth, Joker," Heidi yelled.

He cackled from the kitchen as he scraped down his grill and waited for the mid-morning rush. For some reason, they had a lull between eight and nine a.m. and it was always the time Jackson showed up.

"Hire a competent cook next time. He can't even get a damn order right."

Jackson was asleep when he'd left the man's home earlier. He'd almost called in sick. When he'd woken to Joker coming home last night and asked him to sleep naked beside him, he hadn't expected the man to say yes. It had been years since he'd slept beside a naked man. His ex was a pajama bottoms and t-shirt to bed kind of man. The man had also been slick skinned. Years of manscaping—one stray hair and his ex lost his damn mind. Oh, but not Jackson, and his man was sexy as fuck.

Before he'd left to go to work, he'd taken the time to study every inch of Jackson exposed by the pushed down sheet. The sheer amount of scars had brought tears to his eyes. They were a part of Jackson and as horrific as the damage was, the man was perfection. Lean, powerful muscles under hair-roughened skin covered in thick black hair. The sight of the perfect seven-inch uncut cock in a thick nest of pubes was mouthwatering.

"Dem!"

He smiled sweetly as he stuck his head through the window.

"Hello, baby, you bellowed?"

His man was too cute when he glared and silently threatened bodily harm. If he didn't get a spanking out of this one, he didn't know what else to do.

"What the hell is this shit?"

"That's your breakfast."

Along with Jackson's customary six pancakes, he also made the man scrambled eggs, home fries, and bacon. The man didn't eat enough, and his diet was sorely lacking.

"This isn't what I ordered."

He almost cackled like a madman at the disgust on Jackson's face. He couldn't get over it...the man was adorable.

"Eat it."

"I don't want it."

"Eat it anyway, and I made you lunch to take to work. No arguments. Do as I say."

"I hate you."

"I hate you more."

"You coming home...to the trailer tonight?"

He didn't miss the slight pause and turned as he heard Heidi gasp, he smirked at the shock on her face. He winked at her and turned his attention back to Jackson.

"Do you want me to?"

"It was a fucking yes or no question, not an opening for an interrogation."

"You should know all about interrogations. But to answer your question, yes, I left my stuff there."

Heidi sounded like she was going to choke to death.

"That's why I asked. I nearly tripped over it this morning when I got up. Should I set it on the steps for you?"

"Baby, you're going to hurt my feelings."

"I must try harder since I don't seem to be succeeding."

"Do I have to come out there?"

"No, stay your ass in the kitchen."

He snorted as Joker used his fork to push the second plate away and then tore into the stack of pancakes.

"Both plates better be empty before you leave here."

"You're not the boss of me."

"Are you three?"

Heidi gave up the pretense that she wasn't paying attention and ran into the kitchen loudly laughing when Jackson flipped him off. He straightened and turned to find Heidi wiping tears from her face.

"What am I going to do with him?"

"I have no advice for you, Dem, you picked the meanest man in town."

"But he's so adorable, Heidi."

"You need to get out more."

"I get out plenty. You're going to have to take him this when he pays." He picked up the metal Beast Lunch box he'd picked up while Jackson was away. "It's his lunch."

"I'm not taking him that!"

"Why not?"

"What about him being the meanest man in town didn't you get?"

"It's all show."

"Dem, all kidding aside, you do know about Joker's past, right?"

"I know what I need to know, and unless he wants to tell me more, I don't need to know it. So, I'm going to take my future grouchy husband his lunch." He hooked the handle of the lunchbox on one of the grips and made his way out of the kitchen.

"I was told you were crazy, but I didn't believe it."

"Yeah, yeah, one little incident at Pride involving no clothes, rainbow streamers, and a clown nose and I'm forever known as crazy. "

He approached Jackson's table with a grin on his face. "Hello, Handsome, do you come here often?"

"Before you showed up, I had an enjoyable and blissfully silent breakfast."

He slammed the lunch box down on the table. "There's your lunch," he said as he eased onto the seat opposite Jackson.

"You've got to be fucking joking."

"Nope. Made it special just for you. Also, there's extra in there for Killer."

He'd noticed Jackson's habit of feeding Killer some of his lunch until she was full, and then Jackson would eat the rest. Jackson was covetous of the things and people he considered his. He wondered how many years Jackson went without things and people all his own? He hadn't missed the obsessive neatness of Jackson's surroundings and the way he was protective. He couldn't deny he wanted to belong to Jackson.

"Extra for Killer?"

"Yep."

"Th...thanks."

"You want me to bring dinner when I come?"

"Naw, I'll get some steaks to throw on the grill."

The chime over the door signaled the lull was over. He pushed up on his crutches but didn't leave before leaning down and giving Jackson a quick kiss. As much as he longed to linger, he didn't want to make the man uncomfortable.

He headed back to the kitchen. Taking his perch on the rolling bar stool he used to move around the kitchen. It wasn't ideal, but he wasn't ready to find another job. He loved cooking and knew he could start catering…he just didn't want to give into his body…his limitations yet.

He pushed away those thoughts and focused on better ones. Jackson and dinner. When he'd come to Powers, he hadn't thought about finding someone there. One look at Jackson's scowl in the single picture and knew the man was special. He didn't know if it would go anywhere, and no matter how much he wanted it to, he had to get Jackson to let him in. Everyone left the man alone, let Jackson stay in the past, but he wasn't going to do that.

Jackson Webb was his, and soon the man would know it.

Heidi yelled order, and he got to work. He caught Jackson leaving and smiled at the lunchbox tucked under Jackson's arm. *Good boy*.

"What the hell is this," he asked several hours later as he pulled open the door and threw his bag inside. It landed almost on Jackson's scuffed tactical boots. He'd known getting his man wasn't going to be easy, but Jackson needed to stop being an asshole.

"I left your bag on the steps."

"Don't be obtuse. How was your day?"

He slowly ascended the steps. His legs were tired and his back hurt, but that was normal.

"Same as always."

"Did you eat your lunch?"

"Yes, I ate my lunch."

Jackson was acting strange, not unusual and he knew having him around was new. His man didn't do well with things outside his comfort zone. He was more than willing to be patient. He took a seat on the couch but kept distance between them in case Jackson was not in the mood to be touched. He'd give anything for the man to touch him.

Patience wasn't a virtue he possessed, and it had gotten worse since he'd met Jackson.

"Why do you let them call you Joker? I know you don't like it."

"My friends are idiots, except for Harper, she's perfect."

A thought struck him, and he needed to know.

"Why didn't you ever hook up with Harper or have you?"

He choked back a laugh at Jackson's slow pan toward him. He tried to keep his expression as serious as possible.

"She's like my sister, that's fucked up."

"Most of the people in town thought you had a thing for her."

"She's like my sister."

Having Jackson repeat the sentence like he was an idiot should've offended him, but he was just amused.

"Not even a little attraction?"

"I'm gay, and she's a woman."

"When you put it like that then it does sound silly."

"I tried to take care of her, but I didn't do a very good job of it."

"Harper loves you, and I'm sure she thinks you did a great job."

"I should've killed Bill sooner."

Jackson said it so matter of fact, as if he was talking about the weather, it shocked him a bit. He understood the motive and knew Harper's ex-whatever he was wouldn't have stopped until Gideon and Harper were dead. Jackson had done what was necessary.

"Are you leaving?"

There was a deadness to Jackson's tone. The man expected him to get up and walk away, give up on there being a *them* some time in the future. That wasn't what was going to happen. Jackson was a runner, and everyone else let him be, but that wasn't Dem. He didn't want the other man to feel like the only way to exist was to lock himself away in a shack when the rage became too much to bear.

"I'm not going anywhere. Let me sit a minute, and I'll get dinner started. Where's Killer?"

"In bed taking a nap, she's pissed at me."

"What did you do to our furry daughter?"

"It was her own fault. She rolled in burnt oil, and she needed a bath."

He laughed and leaned sideways and laid his head on Jackson's shoulder. He stayed still until he was sure Jackson wasn't going to pull away. Would there be a time when Jackson became comfortable with affection? It wasn't a guarantee. The man had lived through hell and only time would tell, but he had all the time in the world. He wanted a chance, and he wasn't scared of working for it.

11 Jackson was Losing His Mind

Killer perched on his bent knee and watched every move Dem made. She was quickly becoming accustomed to the man being there. She even let Dem pet her. Dem moved around the kitchen area while Jackson drank his beer.

The memories of the night before tortured him all day. The solid warmth of Dem's body against his and the soft moans every time he shifted against Dem or pulled him closer. He didn't understand how it felt right to have Dem there in his space...his bed. His friends, even Harper wasn't allowed in his place.

He lifted Killer off his knee and placed her on the floor. "Your bed."

She snarled at him and went to her little cubby he'd built under the bed. On the nights his nightmares were bad, he'd make her sleep there. He refused to allow himself to hurt her.

"Door."

She pulled the tiny door closed.

"Nice trick," Dem spoke over his shoulder then went back to putting the leftovers away.

"Turn around," he ordered as he straightened.

Dem turned with a confused expression that twisted his gorgeous features. Dem was perfect. Beyond handsome and he didn't understand why Dem wanted him. What he hid under his clothes wasn't something a man should want or find attractive. He wasn't sexy or charming—he wasn't like his friends who had men falling all over them. The married ones were so in love with their partners it was painful to be around them.

He reached back over his head and removed his t-shirt. It was the moment of truth. He dropped the fabric to the floor and leaned back into the cushions.

"Do you like what you see?"

He studied Dem while the man stared at him. He waited for revulsion. The slightest hint Dem didn't want him. It didn't happen. Dem's lids grew heavy, and Dem leaned back against the counter.

"I love what I see. I got a good look before I went to work this morning."

Dem didn't look away, his gaze moved over him slowly as if the man didn't want to miss an inch of exposed skin.

He didn't look down. He knew every scar by memory. Remembered the pain, the pleas for mercy that fell on deaf ears, and the sadistic pleasure he'd learned Garnet craved. The man had gotten off on it. He had become his mother's surrogate after she'd disappeared. Every lash, brand, cut, was meant for her. He forced away the screams in his ears, hers and his, falling into a perfect duet. Voices raised in the strains of music and pain, harmonized and overlapping. After the torture, Garnet always went out and brought home woman after woman, their screams joined his and his mother's. He'd taken the lashes, knew the scent of blood and infection, and the women took the other horrors Garnet unleashed.

Strange women who still lived in this town. Saw him and saw Garnet. Their hells repeated in their minds just by his presence.

He needed something to replace it. Exchange pain for pleasure. He craved anything to wash away the evil. Cleanse him of the memories of the ones he'd been too young and weak to save—to save his mother.

"Strip for me."

"What's going on, Jackson?"

"I said strip."

He awaited the argument. The nearly guaranteed no he'd accept because he wasn't a monster—no would always mean no. He wouldn't take someone's power—their safety—he knew too well how it felt to be defenseless.

But, he wanted a memory just for himself. A remembrance of being wanted even for a brief moment. To not be the rapist's son. To not be the product of violence. One day soon, he'd be alone again. But at that moment, he wanted to know want and need. Even if he couldn't accept the touch of this man. Touches he'd avoided, fought to save himself from, and he craved to have a person belong to him. To know what his friends probably took for granted. They were allowed to touch and love on their partners, kiss them freely without terror of a remembered lick of flame as he took lash after lash of Garnet's whip. Pain overshadowing everything beyond his instinct to survive.

He held his breath and didn't say a word—didn't move.

Dem crossed his arms and grabbed the bottom of his t-shirt. Perfection exposed in increments—painfully slow seconds as Dem's shirt ascended. The shirt disappeared, but he couldn't look away from the smooth tanned skin of Dem's torso. Dem's stomach was firm, but not defined by rippling abs. His gaze moved up to a powerful chest and round, beaded nipples.

He tried not to compare himself to Dem. He was nowhere near skinny, but he also wasn't built like some bodybuilder. His stomach was covered in hair and bore a slight paunch. That slight softness didn't compare to the scars and Dem hadn't seen them all yet.

"What do you want, Jackson? Whatever it is it's yours."

Dem's softly spoken words caused him to jerk his gaze to the man's face. Gorgeous. He wondered if what Dem said was true. He'd tried so many times to be normal.

"I don't know."

"Can I ask you something?"

He nodded because he didn't think he could speak with his throat closing up, panic took over the closer he came to the edge of his comfort zone.

"Have you done this before."

"I don't fuck."

"That's good because our first time isn't going to be fucking. Without thinking or second guessing, what do you want right now?"

"To watch you get off for me."

"Nothing else. Don't want me to touch you…to make you—"

"I don't need it. I just want the memory for when you're gone."

He couldn't miss Dem's flinch at his harsh words, but they were true. He didn't expect Dem to stick around longer than whatever fucked up fascination Dem had with him. The man slept in his arms. He'd have that, but he wanted—needed something more. He wanted to hear Dem call his name as he came. Tuck it away. A secret that was his and for no one else to know.

He didn't want touch, he wanted to watch and memorize the details. Count every breath, moan, whimper, and heavy-lidded look. He was almost forty years old, and he needed to experience what it was like to be wanted at least once. What if he was like Garnet and he couldn't take no for an answer? What if he hurt Dem? He wouldn't allow that; it was the reason they could never fuck.

"Where do you want me?"

"In my bed."

He stayed seated as Dem slipped his arms into his crutches then made his way to the bedroom. It wasn't a long wait. His place was tiny and meant for one person. He pushed to his feet as he caught sight of Dem taking a seat on the edge of the mattress. The man worked his jeans off and dropped them to the floor.

"If I do this, give you this one thing, you need to give me something."

"What," he asked as he took in the hard, slender cock, the head flushed dark pink and resting on thin, hairy thighs. Dem legs had muscle definition, but nowhere near that of Dem's upper body.

"I want you naked and on the bed with me. If I can't touch you, then I need you close. Please."

There was strain etched around the man's full lips. Dem's eyes were brighter like when he laughed—but different—sadder. He didn't want that. He was damaged goods. Selfish for demanding this one thing. Did Dem know tonight would be it? That tomorrow he would force Dem to leave him alone. This one request would break him. He couldn't look at Dem and remember what he'd demanded—witnessed—and know Dem would never be his. What they had wouldn't be normal.

"Jackson, if tonight is all I get, please just give me this one thing."

He couldn't deny Dem. He knew he should stop it now and walk away before it went too far, but he craved it—like his next breath. He forced his hands not to shake as he undid the button of his jeans, slid the zipper down, and the erection he'd just had disappeared. He pushed the denim over his hips and lower until he lifted his feet to remove his pants.

He inhaled deeply through his nose and exhaled through his mouth as he straightened. Dem's gaze moved over him, from head to toe, then back to his groin. He knew what Dem saw. The scars along his hips and on his cock from the tip of the whip as it had wrapped around his body. The circular scars of cigars and cigarettes. He made a simple mistake of looking too long at a boy in the grocery store. Garnet promised to make a man out of him.

The pain had been excruciating. He'd passed out several times only to awaken—

"Jackson," Dem called his name.

He refused to look at Dem.

"You still won't let me touch you?"

"I don't want to get used to something I can't keep."

"Who says you can't keep me?"

He stared at his toes, avoided looking at anything else. His dick hung flaccid, and he was embarrassed by it. He started to lean down and reach for his pants.

"You're meant for someone better than me."

Strong hands grabbed his face and jerked his head up. He stared into watery eyes and tears slipped down Dem's cheeks.

"There's no one better. No one, Jackson."

He tried not to flinch but failed when soft wet lips touched his. Dem tasted of tears. He clenched his fists on his knees and forced himself not to reach out.

"Give us a chance. I don't expect you to kiss me in public or walk down the street holding my hand. We have plenty of time for that. Just let me touch you. Nothing else. We don't have to have sex, make love, or as you put it, fuck. What happens in this bed is just us. No specters of a dead man. You and me."

Dem's hands left his face and wrapped around his wrists, pulling him toward Dem. He straightened as their mouths lost contact.

He stood between Dem's parted thighs and gentle lips brushed one scar after another. He closed his eyes, refused to watch just in case he saw something other than desire in Dem's eyes. Even as Dem kissed every inch of skin he could reach, he waited for the retreat—the rejection.

Seconds turned into minutes, and Dem's hands joined in and gripped his hips.

"You can touch me."

He let out a shuddered sigh as he raised his shaking hands and combed his fingers through the softness of Dem's long hair. The strands teased his skin. His cock firmed against Dem's chest.

"Did you still want to watch me stroke my cock for you?"

"Yes."

"What else do you want?"

What else? He wanted so much, but he went with what he could have now.

He pushed Dem onto the bed and then helped Dem until the man's head rested on the pillows. Nervousness caused a lump to form in his throat as he turned to his dresser. He pulled opened the top drawer and pulled out the items he needed.

He was a bastard, jumped into fights with armed men without second thoughts, but this was something else. He couldn't fuck Dem and trust himself—maybe never could. He'd keep that to himself.

He tossed the dildo, condom and lube on the bed next to Dem's hip. The man was sprawled on his bed. A temptation and every one of his dreams rolled into one. Dem's full lips were curled into a half smile. Dem's jaw was covered in a few days' worth of stubble.

"You want me to use that?"

"Yes."

"Have you ever—"

"No, I tried, but couldn't." He bought it a year ago when he'd gone out of town, and as much as he'd tried to make himself relax, he couldn't do it. It was almost as awkward as when he tried to jerk off.

"That's fine, not everyone likes anal. It's completely normal."

He wanted to believe Dem, but he'd heard the stories, even walked in on some of his friends fucking, and it hadn't seemed forced. He hadn't stayed long, but the screams and pleas for more kind of clued him in.

"Come here." Dem opened his legs wide.

He crawled onto the bed and sat back on his heels.

"We're going to take this slow and at your pace. You're in charge."

"Of course I am."

Dem rolled his eyes.

He was all show at the moment. He didn't know what he was doing or what to expect.

Apparently, that didn't matter, Dem kept his eyes on him, then Dem's hands began to move over his own chest. Dem pinched his nipples and his back arched, a deep groan and the rustle of skin against cotton filled the silence.

His cock hardened at the picture Dem made. The man's tanned skin flushed and misted with sweat. His heartbeat quickened as Dem wrapped his hand around his dick and stroked, base to tip. When Dem reached the head, he rolled his palm over it. The movements slow and sensual. Dem eyelids lowered, but he didn't close them.

He fisted his hands on his thighs. He remembered the warm silk of Dem's skin against his. He jerked his gaze to Dem as he heard the snick of the lid of the lube. Dem slicked his fingers and brought them to his own hole.

He clenched his teeth as he observed Dem pushing one finger inside, then Dem worked his way up to two and three.

"What are you imagining?"

"You, your cock instead of my fingers. You'd feel so much better, Jackson, so—"

Dem paused as he rolled his hips, fucked himself onto the digits. He wrapped his hands around his own cock and stroked, he jerked as ecstasy coursed through his veins for the first time.

He wished he was different.

"Put a condom on it and fuck me."

"I don't—"

"You don't have to touch me, baby."

He hands shook as he reached for the pale colored dildo and quickly readied it with the condom and more lube.

"Where did you get the condom and lube?"

"Don't be jealous, I stole them from the Twin's supply drop."

"I wasn't."

He knew Dem lied. He pressed the flared head to Dem's stretched hole and pushed.

"I want hard and fast, and when you cum, I want it on my skin."

He gave a jerky nod and slammed into Dem, causing Dem to push his head into the pillow. The harder he pounded the toy into Dem, the louder the man's grunts and whimpers became. Dem writhed and pulled his legs back to his chest, opening himself to take more. He synced his movements with the thrust and retreat, gripped his cock tight and imagined he was inside Dem. Taking him.

"Fuck, I thought…about this so many times."

"Did you want me to fuck you?"

"Y—yes."

"How did you want it?"

"Like I'm not weak."

He froze at the tears in Dem's eyes. He didn't like that, and he leaned over Dem. What did he know about comfort? He kissed Dem's closed eyes.

"Weak, explain."

"Everyone has always been gentle with me. I wanted passion and heat, out of control. No one has ever—"

He snapped his wrist and drove the toy harder into Dem. His wrist pushed to Dem's tight balls, felt them roll against his skin. His mouth hovered over Dem's, and the man's high-pitched grunts warmed his lips. He slammed into Dem harder and faster, heat and something dangerous unfurled in his chest.

"Like that?"

"Yes. Make it hurt, please, Jackson."

"I can't—"

"You and me, baby, only us, what we want…no one else."

He jerked the toy from Dem, threw it aside and flipped the man over. He slammed into Dem and heat and pressure engulfed his dick.

He blanketed Dem's back and pressed his lips to Dem's ear.

"Hurt?"

"Y—yes."

His weight pushed Dem flat onto the mattress. His thighs pushed at the back of Dem's. He took Dem's wrists in his hands and pressed them into the mattress. Dem bucked and screamed, the harder he took Dem, the more the man begged for it.

"Tell me you want me," he demanded.

"I want you."

He lifted and looked between them, Dem's skin abraded by the hair on his chest. His hole inflamed and stretched tight around his bare cock. He watched his shaft disappear into Dem with brutal thrusts. He should slow down, be more gentle, but Dem's skin was slick and hot against his. His face flushed and beautiful, drawn and locked in the space between pain and pleasure.

"Only my cock, no one else, mine. No one takes what's…" He slammed forward hard enough to move Dem up the bed. "Mine. Understand?"

"Shit, don't fucking stop."

Dem screamed, and he wanted to hear it again. He rode Dem until the man shook so hard it nearly threw him off. He owned Dem, every inch, his tight hole and his beautiful body. It was his—Dem was his.

"Cum, now." He thrust and retreated in sharp jabs of his hips.

Dem's upper body bowed. He sunk his teeth into Dem's shoulder as Dem's ass clenched down to the point of pain. He surged upward to watch Dem fuck himself onto his cock. Took him until Dem collapsed. He pulled out and leaned over Dem. His fingers fisted in Dem's hair as he turned the man to look at him. Dem's eyes were rolled back, and he slammed his mouth down onto Dem's as he stroked his dick. He worked himself in a rough, painful rhythm.

"You want my cum on your sore little hole. You let me use it like a good boy."

It was all his twisted fantasies rolled into one. The things he hid and denied, but it was the first time he didn't notice the scars and no memories tortured him.

He groaned into Dem's mouth as he came and spilled onto Dem's pert, round ass. He didn't stop until he'd wrung the last of it, and he placed his forearms on either side of Dem's head. He grunted as he rubbed against Dem.

Dem ran shaking fingers through his hair and scored his scalp with his short nails.

"Are you still telling me goodbye?"

"Yes."

Dem nodded, and he tried to ignore Dem's small sob. He was a bastard. After that, he just proved Dem wasn't for him. He couldn't let it happen again. He closed his eyes and pressed his forehead to Dem's nape.

"I'm...I'm sorry."

"Jackson, don't be sorry. It'll be okay, I promise."

It wouldn't be okay. Nothing ever would be again. He'd had one taste of what he'd always secretly wanted, and he had to let him go. One night would have to last the rest of his life.

12 Dem had Felt Whole for Once

He'd locked himself in his room since he'd left Jackson's two days before. Only left to go to work. What was even more painful than the morning after the goodbye…Jackson hadn't come in for breakfast. He looked for him. Jackson probably wouldn't talk to him, but he wanted to see him.

For one night, he'd felt whole and normal as if his body wasn't slowly failing him. He was still sore. Still felt Jackson inside him. Never once in almost forty years had he ever let anyone take him without a condom, but if he had only the one night, he'd wanted it. Jackson made him feel like he was normal and not the fun-loving guy with the arm crutches.

His parents hadn't treated him as if he had a disability, so the real world had proved a rude awakening. He'd done everything he had wanted to in life with only their encouragement. His head popped up from the pillow at the soft knock.

"Dem, can I come in?"

Harper's voice was soft and concerned, he could hear it. She'd tried to get him to talk several times over the last few days, but all he'd wanted was silence.

"Gideon had a show at Brawlers, so he isn't here."

"Come in."

The door opened, and Harper stepped in, closing it behind her.

"Are you okay?"

"No."

"Joker didn't mean to do whatever he did."

He despised the fact everyone always instantly defended Jackson as if he'd done something wrong. The man had reasons for being the way he was. Jackson had survived something most people wouldn't, and even if Jackson told him goodbye, Jackson had given him a gift. A night where he wasn't treated as if he were fragile.

"He didn't do anything wrong, Harper. Do people always assume the worst about him?"

"I don't assume the worst. Joker has taken care of me the best he could for a long time. People might think he's crazy, but he's my best friend."

He pushed up to lean back against the headboard as Harper took a seat on the end of the bed.

"Why didn't anyone help him?"

"Has he told you?"

"I didn't have to be told. I saw. Who the hell would do that to a kid, hell, an adult?"

"Garnet Senior and Junior, there were stories that Senior was a nice kid, well liked in Powers, maybe a little odd. But small towns have at least one eccentric. He left town for a while and came back with a wife. Peaches said she was a pretty woman if a little quiet. Senior built a house out in the middle of nowhere. When Junior turned five, the wife suddenly killed herself. No explanations."

"She did it to escape."

Harper nodded. "After she died, people started talking. They didn't remember seeing a lot of her, but when she came into town, she was timid…sometimes had bruises."

"Again, why didn't anyone do anything?"

"The same family has been the law in this town until Pelter took over. They tended to look the other way as long as you were—"

"White?"

"We don't have the proudest history for tolerance. Back in the sixties, a group bought some land. Very peace and love, and shook things up around here.

"Peaches and Gib moved back to town and opened the shop. Lily and Damon moved here. After a while, the good people outnumbered the bad ones, but to be honest, the bad ones were in power."

"Do you think Jackson's mom did the same as his grandmother?"

"I don't know. Jackson doesn't talk about it. The only reason I know is because he used to talk to me when he thought I was asleep. Told me the things Garnet did to him.

"Did he hurt you," Harper asked with a hint of embarrassment.

He placed his hand on her forearm and gave it a squeezed. "Not in the way you think. He wanted something, and I was more than willing to give it to him, but I made demands of my own. Did he go back out to the shack?"

"Why?"

"He hasn't been in for breakfast, and he likes his routine."

"I don't know where he is. Sin and Saint did a flyover, but there was no sign of him. Do you want him?"

Had his mind changed? No, he wanted Jackson just as much as the first time he'd seen the man's picture or when Jackson was arrested in front of the diner. Nothing had changed, to be honest, he wanted Jackson more.

"Since the first time I saw him."

"What about him did it for you?"

"What doesn't?"

"Let's narrow it down."

Harper smiled as she turned and crossed her legs on the bed, her forearms rested on her thighs. He'd quickly fell in love with Harper. She was all sweetness and light. He knew from the stories that hadn't always been her, yet he didn't know any different than the Harper who sat across from him.

"I know what he wants, but he doesn't think he deserves it. He's handsome of course. The whole bastard attitude, I like that. He makes me feel normal."

"Normal? I don't know if that is an insult or not."

"Not like that. He doesn't treat me like I'm damaged. I don't know if he even pays attention to the crutches. Yeah, he modified his bike to make it easier for me to ride, but he doesn't try to coddle me. He didn't treat me like I was breakable."

"He wouldn't think of doing anything like that."

"Everyone else does. Even Gideon does it sometimes. Asks if I need help to my room. We've known each other so long I don't pay attention to it. Mainly, I don't want someone who dates me to treat me less than."

"Why would they treat you less than?"

"I want equal in everything from everyday relationship stuff to the bedroom. He gave me what I wanted."

"You two had sex?"

Her eyes were comically wide.

"He touched you and let you touch him?"

"It didn't start out that way. It was going to be a little mutual masturbation, but Jackson lost control a bit. You'd be surprised, he's pretty impeccable at dirty talk."

"I'm not hearing this." She slapped her hands over her ears and started humming loudly.

He couldn't keep himself from laughing at the horror on her face. He leaned forward and removed her hands from her ears. "I asked him did you two ever hook up?"

"He's like my brother, that's…disgusting."

"He had the same reaction, but for a minute or two I was jealous."

"Of me?"

"Yes, you. You're beautiful, and you two have been close. I also heard rumors that you two were together."

"No, best friends. He's always been hyper-protective, but he's that way with most of the women and children in town."

"Because of his past?"

"I think a part of him feels guilty about his mom, but how can an eight-year-old protect himself and his mother?"

"Do you think I should let him go?"

"No," Harper said sharply. "Everyone lets Joker do what he wants. When he disappears, they leave him alone. We love him, but we're used to him and his…quirks. If you want him, you're going to have to fight a lifetime of conditioning. I can't believe I'm going to ask this."

"I'm an open book, Harper, there's not much I won't answer."

"When you two, ya know…" Harper paused, and her face blazed with mortification.

"Had sex?"

"Yes, that. Was it gentle or, ya know…" She stopped again.

"You want to know if the sex was rough?"

"I can't believe we're having this conversation."

"You brought it up."

"He was a product of non-consensual sex."

"He told me, but he couldn't think—" He'd known, but it hadn't crossed his mind until Harper brought it up that Jackson might relate all sex to rape or—

He was horrified by the thought, even more so that Jackson would ever consider what they did non-consensual.

He understood Jackson's fear, but still didn't—he'd begged for Jackson to take him.

How did someone live with the knowledge that they came to be by the vilest act?

"Joker doesn't know what a healthy sex life is, Dem. If it got rough and, in his mind after the afterglow, he starts second guessing. Thinks what if you in some way said no—"

He didn't even know what to say, and then it hit him. Jackson had been rough with him. Held him down. Took him raw and bare. Jackson associated all sex with—Dem bit his lip as tears again burned his eyes and slipped down his cheeks. Jackson saw himself as a monster. Believed himself to be just like Garnet and that was the farthest thing from the truth. What they did was mutual. He wasn't forced.

He asked for what he wanted, and Jackson gave it to him. There wasn't anything wrong with what they did together.

"He thinks he's exactly like the bastard?"

"Yes, he lives in an almost constant rage. Ready to defend himself at any moment. At sixteen, he beat Garnet to death, they sentenced him as an adult, and he went to an adult prison. He's been in a violent environment since before birth. He thinks he's damaged and unworthy."

"He's not. He did what was necessary. Did they see what was done to him?"

"He was tried here in Powers and convicted here."

"That doesn't make it right."

"I didn't say it did, but he also found his mother's journals. She outlined everything Garnet did to her since the day he grabbed her off the side of the road. Every beating, lashing, even rape was written, and Joker read them repeatedly. He admitted he found the journals years before, and they took that as a sign the murder was premeditated."

"Where would he be?"

"If he's not at the shack or at home, I don't know. I know sometimes he gets in his truck or on his bike and just drives…clears his head. He normally checks in with me, though, so I don't worry."

"He hasn't done that?"

"No."

"What should I do?"

"Wait for him to come home. It's the only thing you can do. If Joker doesn't want to be found, then you won't find him. I'm going to bed and read, I don't like when Gideon isn't home."

"You two are really cute together."

"I love him. He's never tried to change me. He's always made me feel safe. Gave me choices. He wants to have kids with me."

"And have you two decided yet?"

He was thankful for the change of subject, he'd had enough heavy to last him for a while.

"Lou, Linus' sister, she acted as a surrogate for Lucky and Priest, and offered to do the same for us."

"That's amazing."

"Gideon wants me—"

"He wants some little blonde beauties running around the farm?"

"Yeah. I don't know, I'd kinda like some handsome little Gingers running around."

"Do both."

"I don't know about that. I'd be happy with one."

"You two will work it out. Either way, you two will be so great as parents."

"Do you think so?"

"Positive."

"Thanks, Dem." Harper stood and straightened her plain white gown. "Give Joker a few more days. If anyone knows where he is, it's Peaches. She's his lawyer, so if he's in trouble, he'd definitely call her."

"I have some thinking to do before I try to claim my man anyway."

"Don't talk yourself out of it."

"Never, I just need to make sure I do this right. Jackson has been alone for a long time, and I'm trying to move into his personal space. I just need to woo him a bit."

"How are you going to do that?"

"I'm going to call my mother."

"Good luck with that."

He waited until Harper left and closed the door, then he laid back down, staring up at the ceiling. His brain tried to process all he'd learned from Harper. He hadn't wondered why Jackson killed Garnet passed the obvious abuse. Was there more than the torture? He'd seen the scars on Jackson's penis. The circular ones that couldn't be made by anything other than cigars or cigarettes being put on his groin. He couldn't imagine the pain and suffering Jackson went through the first sixteen years of his life. What could've happened to him in an adult prison?

The what ifs were stacking up, and he hated them. He hated he couldn't be with Jackson. He couldn't say he loved Jackson, but he knew he could. He cared for and wanted Jackson. It wouldn't be easy, but he knew anything that was easy wasn't worth having. The struggle made it worth it. He needed to wait out Jackson's panic, and when the man surfaced, he'd make sure Jackson knew that nothing Jackson did was unwanted.

13 Broken Ribs and a Jail Cell

"You ready to tell me what the hell is wrong with you, Joker," Pelter asked for the tenth time since the man had pulled him over coming back into town.

He shifted on the uncomfortable cot, and his broken ribs weren't cooperating. It had been awhile since someone got the jump on him, but when he decided to take on ten pissed off bikers for harassing a waitress in a Virginia diner a week before, he hadn't exactly been thinking straight. Luckily, the cops thought he was outnumbered, and he'd stood up for someone so they'd let him go. Killer hadn't been happy when he came back to the room several hours passed her dinner time.

She hadn't left his pocket unless necessary since. Right then, she was a light weight on his stomach with her head sticking out the hole at the top of the pocket.

Peaches wasn't going to be happy with him when she found out he fucked up. Hopefully, Harper wouldn't be mad too. Killer and Peaches were enough.

"Dem filed a missing person report."

He jerked his head up and stared at Pelter. He'd only been gone a little over three weeks. It wasn't unusual for him to take off to clear his head. No one even acknowledged his absences. The fact Dem had, shocked him a bit. He'd told the man goodbye. They couldn't be together, Dem was way too good for him. What he'd done to Dem should've been proof enough.

"You heard that right, he filed one three days ago when no one seemed to know where you were. That man isn't looking too good."

He tried not to care, but no matter how far he'd ridden, nothing could banish the visions of Dem in his bed. He watched the man sleep all night. Everything in him screamed to keep him. Instead, he'd told Dem bye and walked away.

The first time in his life he'd freely touched someone, and he'd treated Dem like a whore. Dem hadn't complained, had begged him to be rough, but why couldn't he be gentle? He cared. He wondered what it would be like to claim Dem like his friends did their men.

He wasn't in the closet. He never had sex before, but that didn't make him any less gay. It didn't seem right until he had Dem underneath him in his bed.

"Is he okay?"

"Do you even care?"

"Cut the shit, Pelter, tell me."

"He's worried to death about you. Last I heard, he was living at your place. Also, he reorganized your office and cleaned out all the paperwork. He's also sporting a lot of hoodies the last few weeks."

Something about Dem in his clothes made him feel even more possessive than he had before. He needed Dem, the man belonged to him, but he didn't know if he could keep him. Dem could be taken from him. The man would find someone else gentler and better. He refused to ruin the man's life.

He shouldn't like the fact Dem decided to make himself at home in his trailer.

"I—"

"I know you hate when I mention it, but I read your file. A competent legal system would've thrown out the murder charges on you. You didn't do anything wrong, and you're punishing yourself for shit that wasn't your fault. Do you have any idea how fucking lucky you are? You got a chance with a man that's pretty great. Understanding as hell if he wants to be with your grumpy ass and what the fuck do you do? You take off without a damn word."

"This isn't any—"

"I'm making it my business, some of us would kill for what you got; a chance at something and you're fucking it up."

"I don't have a chance."

"Do you know what I'd give to have someone care half as much? I know what it's like, Joker. Most of my family is made of people I'd bust in a heartbeat. Then I live here, and I have to live down the former Sheriff's corruption, deal with the small portion of the populace that doesn't think a black man should be the law around here, throw in the fact that they sure as hell wouldn't want a gay, black Sheriff."

"What about the twins?"

"You know I'm old enough to be their dad, right?"

"Fuck that shit, age ain't got nothing to do with it."

He was glad to be off the topic of Dem for now, but he knew it would come back up sooner or later.

"It has everything to do with it. I already have issues in town, I don't need to toss dating pretty, white twins into the mess."

The corners of his mouth twitched.

"Yeah, find it funny, asshole. I've been single a long time because of my job and the hours, I can do just fine staying single."

"Was there ever a report made on my mother's disappearance?"

"Not that I saw. I did ask around about it. Peaches filled me in that one day your mother just disappeared, and her husband said she ran away. Seems Thorpe was fine with that answer. Your mother was twenty-one with barely any education or work experience, she had a son by all accounts she lived for. Me, I'd think it was suspect."

"Could she have just left?"

"I don't know, but thirty years is a long time to stay away."

"I think the same."

"If you want, I can contact Linus, there isn't much Pure and Hunter can't find."

"No, what if she wants to stay gone?"

"If she's out there, I'm sure if she knew you were looking for her, she'd want to find you. She'd only be probably fifty-one now. You're more equipped than anyone to know what she went through."

"If she is alive, I just hope she's happy."

"If she is alive, maybe even after three decades, you can give her closure knowing the bastard who abused her is dead.

"Let's get you out of here. You've got Dem worried to death."

"Can I just stay in here?"

"No, you can't. I need room for the real criminals, you know the litterers and peeping toms."

"You want a murder or two?"

"Fuck that, I had enough of that before I came here. My life would be so much quieter if you'd behave. Breaking up bar fights and shit isn't my idea of a good time."

He slowly rolled off the cot and got to his feet, and groaned at the discomfort in his ribs. "If you'd give the Twins a call I'm sure they'd set you up with a good time."

"Get the fuck out."

"Just saying, man, they got it bad."

"Quit stalling and go home."

"I'm going."

"King's out front with Ghost to help get you home. You're in no damn condition to ride."

"I got to Powers just fine."

"Take my advice and let them help. King will take you in his truck and Ghost will ride your bike."

He nodded and passed when Pelter stepped out of the way.

"Joker, I know we ain't exactly friends, but you need anything you know how to get in touch. I'm not Thorpe, shit he pulled definitely won't be going on around here anymore."

He didn't say anything, just made his way toward the nearest exit. He strode outside to find King and Ghost leaned back against King's truck. Help wasn't something he asked for, and he wouldn't be starting anytime soon. His ribs were fucked so he'd take the ride. Killer ducked back into the pocket to completely hide herself.

"Finally showed your ass up." King pushed away from the vehicle.

"I'm standing here, ain't I?"

"We should kick your ass, man, you worried the hell out of Dem."

Ghost looked pissed, and he was the calmest man around.

"I needed space."

King just stood back and let Ghost do all the talking, which wasn't unusual. Except for when King was looking for a fuck for the night, the man was quiet.

"It isn't just you, Joker. We're your damn family, and you can't pull this shit. We know you and are used to your bullshit, but Dem doesn't know."

"I made it clear there wasn't anything going to happen."

"So you're just going to fuck him and move on like it was nothing. First person who you let touch you, and you're going to say goodbye like he's nothing?"

"I'm not right for him."

"You're going to go home, and you're going to make this shit right. You've upset my wife too."

That was a low one, he'd never do anything to hurt Harper. She was his best friend and the only one who truly understood him.

He didn't say anything as he jogged around the truck, pulled open the door, and he slid into the passenger seat. King quickly joined him as he listened to his bike start up.

"You know you're fucking up a good thing, right?"

"Don't you start too. I ain't got time."

"All we have is time, and you want to go it alone or do you want someone in your damn corner? Not everyone gets lucky enough to have the one they want. Do the rest of us a favor and show us we got a damn chance."

Luckily King shut up, and they made the rest of the drive in silence. He knew his friend had a thing for Linc, King's ex-brother-in-law, but King didn't have any confidence that Linc would return whatever feelings King had.

They pulled up in front of his shop, and Ghost parked his bike on the sidewalk near his office.

"Do the right thing, Joker, and not what you assume is right," King said without looking at him.

He got out, and Ghost took his place, neither man said anything, and they pulled off leaving him standing there.

He turned his head to glance down the alley to his darkened trailer. Dem's rental sedan was parked behind his truck. Dem was there, in his home, and he hadn't expected it. Everyone always left him alone. Walked away to give him his space; no one had stayed before. He didn't know how to handle that. He held onto the things that were his, home, shop, Killer, yet did he have someone else to call his own? Would Dem be able to handle his rage and nightmares, the parts of him that were broken with no hope of repair?

It was a short walk to his trailer. He only paused long enough to open the door and ascend the steps. He removed Killer from his pocket and set her on the floor.

He took the three long strides that brought him to the bedroom door. Dem was curled up in the middle of his bed, a pillow hugged to his chest, and soft snores filled the small space. The streetlights through the blinds illuminated Dem's face, and he couldn't miss the dark circles under

Dem's eyes or the fact it looked like the man lost a little weight. He'd done that.

Killer took the steps up to the bed and found her spot on the pillow next to Dem. He removed his clothes down to his boxer briefs and crawled onto the bed. The sheet remained between their bodies, no matter how much he needed to feel Dem's skin against his, he wouldn't allow it. He didn't hold Dem or bury his face in Dem's soft hair, he simply laid beside him.

That right there was all that he'd wanted. He had hidden it so well over the years. Kept himself from the temptation, it hadn't turned out to be hard since no one before Dem had ever made him need. Dem made him forget the pain. The rage. For brief moments, he experienced what he thought it was to be normal and whole.

He crossed his arms over his stomach and closed his eyes. Outside of guilt for his mother and the unknown of what happened to her, he knew it wouldn't compare to what he'd done to Dem. He didn't know if an I'm sorry was enough and hoped it would be because it was all he had.

14 Joker Came Home

Everything he had hurt. Dem stretched and instantly became aware of the body behind him. Joker came home. He opened his eyes to see the tiny ball of fur on the pillow next to him. Killer's little face partially hidden by the folds of the pillowcase. She wasn't wearing her usual hoodie or t-shirt. He didn't reach up to pet her in case she hadn't fallen asleep long ago.

He shifted his aching body and hated the twinges in his hips. He hadn't done his stretches the way he was supposed to and worked every hour Heidi would let him. Working made the hours pass quicker, but not fast enough. He sighed as he looked at Jackson, the man hugged himself, and his eyes were wet. His lips moved in his sleep, but nothing came out. His cries were silent.

How many years had Jackson comforted himself through nightmares? He was pissed at Jackson, but he partially understood. He tugged the lightweight blanket over Jackson, and the man's skin was cool and clammy where it brushed his forearm.

The worst part of Jackson's time away was Dem found the box of journals, a bright orange evidence seal broken on an old cardboard box. His curiosity took over, and he'd looked inside, stacks of pictures that showed the crime scene and an emaciated Jackson. His body riddled with fresh scars, wounds oozed with infection, and hands and face covered in blood. He'd read every piece of paper inside. Evidence that only stated Jackson was a danger to society, recommendations for life in prison, and not one said anything about the hell a sixteen-year-old kid went through.

They hadn't taken into account the sadistic torture Jackson endured and survived countless times over his short life. No, they only cared about the fights he'd gotten into and the reports of underage drinking and drugs.

He tentatively raised his hand and placed it on Jackson's cheek, then he closed the inches that separated them. He kissed the salt-tinged flavor of his lips. Jackson had been so close to not being there. Jackson could've succumbed to any of the acts done to him, but he hadn't—he survived it all.

The journals were just as bad, she'd outlined every day of her life for almost nine years. Garnet did the same things he had done to Jackson, the whippings, the beatings, but she'd been subjected to repeated rapes. It had killed him to read it, and he wondered how Mary and Jackson had lived. He couldn't even imagine.

He opened his eyes that had fallen closed as he'd kissed Jackson and found Jackson watching him. Jackson's eyes were filled with tears.

"I'm sorry," Jackson's voice trembled.

"It's okay, we'll deal with it later, all that matters is you're home now."

"I made you cry before I left. I hurt you."

"You didn't do anything wrong."

He'd realized something after Jackson left. When Jackson looked at himself, he saw Garnet. The pictures in the file of Garnet showed them to be nearly identical. To have to look in the mirror and see a mirror image of your abuser every day had to be torture in itself. Jackson didn't possess any healthy examples of sex.

"I took you raw without anything between us, I—"

"Jackson, things got a little out of hand, and we both lost our minds for a minute, but I enjoyed every minute of us together."

"I shouldn't have said the things I did."

"What did I tell you? This was us, you and me, no one else in bed with us not even a memory. You're not him, Jackson. Maybe next time we can do it all gentle."

"You still want to be with me?"

"I'm not exactly happy with you for leaving without a word and staying away so long, but it happened. It's in the past, we work from this moment forward."

Jackson gave a jerky nod.

"Why weren't you under the covers?"

"I didn't know if it would be okay to touch you."

"It's always okay for you to touch me, especially when we're in bed."

He shifted away as Jackson rolled and wiggled until Jackson was under the covers. He couldn't help when he moaned and pushed closer when Jackson's hairy skin touched his. Damn, he'd forgotten how good and right Jackson felt being that close to him.

"How long have you been here?"

"Since about four days after you disappeared. Your office was a disaster. Did you know you had almost a year of paperwork that hadn't been entered into your accounting program?"

"Is that all?"

"Don't tell me there's more."

"I just thought there was more."

"How do you handle your accounting and taxes and all that?"

"My accountant hates me."

"I don't blame him. I started to hate you too, and I only spent a week in your office."

Jackson placed his arm over him and splayed his calloused hand between his shoulder blades.

"Don't you have to be at work," Jackson asked against the side of his throat.

"No, Heidi has barred me from working for the next few days. I wouldn't take my days off, and my body is paying for it."

"What's wrong?"

"All the surgeries I've had over the years to repair the malformations of my hips and pelvis have taken their toll. I have arthritis, and I'm more metal than bone."

"What happened?"

"They don't know, just didn't form right. No cause, mom was healthy, no history of deformities in either family. Just one of those things. The last surgery was when I'd stopped growing to put in permanent pins and plates. Don't treat me different, okay?"

"Why would I treat you different?"

"Because my body isn't—"

"Your body is gorgeous."

"My legs are losing more muscle the less I'm able to stand on them."

"Lay back."

He didn't ask questions just rolled to his back and watched as Jackson got up, then straddled his calves. The covers disappeared and strong, yet surprisingly gentle hands spread out over his pelvis. He bit his lip as Jackson began to massage his pelvis, hips, and down his thighs, then repeated. It was heaven and hell, perfect, just the right amount of pressure. He couldn't keep his body from reacting to Jackson's hands on him. It seemed like forever, but it had only been three weeks.

He didn't call attention to it. He knew things hadn't gone well last time, and they needed to take their time.

"The idea of sex always felt wrong," Jackson spoke but didn't stop with the massage.

"What was wrong about it?"

"I read the journals, knew what he'd done, but I also remember the women he'd bring home and the way they screamed. I knew I was gay early, but also if Garnet ever found out, I'd be dead. I looked at a boy once when I was a kid, he was about my age...he was pretty, and I didn't understand it then but a little feminine. Garnet caught me. He used my groin for a fucking ashtray. I didn't know about anything sex positive, but—"

"But what?"

"You can't be around the crews and not walk in on something, the partners always seem—"

"Turned on, enjoying themselves?"

"Yeah, those. Did Ghost ever tell you I went after him when I heard Harper scream one time?"

"No, but I bet that was awkward."

"She was embarrassed and wouldn't look at me, but I thought—"

"You thought your friend was hurting her? Were you having a flashback?"

Jackson sat back and raised his hands to scrub over his face. "Why are you still here?"

"Because you're worth me being here. Just don't pull the disappearing bullshit again. Peaches is also way more pissed than I am."

"Shit, was she here?"

"Yep, came by to discuss something with you when I told her you were missing for more than a week. For a sweet looking lady despite the tattoos, she has one helluva mouth on her."

"Fuck."

"You're terrified of Peaches?"

"Damn right, she has friends in very low places, ones that make me look like a sweetheart. She worked as a public defender and a defense attorney for a long time. Peaches didn't survive with her client list without being tough."

He smiled as Jackson fell to the side and stared up at the ceiling. Jackson's hands scrubbed over his face.

"So, we're safe in assuming, you're fucked right now?"

"So fucked. And everyone will know I'm home because my asshole friends are gossips."

"Want me to go make coffee?"

"No." Jackson rolled over and laid his arm over him. "Stay. I'm safe until at least noon."

He placed his arm over Jackson's and laced their fingers together.

"Tell me about your trip."

Jackson did, and he laid there listening, shaking his head. Jackson needed a keeper, and it was a good thing he was up to the task.

15 She Might Be Alive

She might be alive—those words went through Jackson like an high-voltage shock. He'd never thought he'd hear that. Over the years, he had wished for her to be at peace whether that was alive or dead. He didn't say a word as he looked across the conference room table at Trenton Security Headquarters.

Peaches and Pure had a file open in front of them. Pure was a mind-bending physical contradiction to the woman beside him. Pure was huge, broad with tanned skin free of ink. Peaches was covered in ink from her neck down, in a power suit the woman was a force to be reckoned with in court; Peaches was just a force. Pure was one of those guys while built on a massive scale, he had a softness to him that showed his gentle giant nature. Boyish, All-American looks, the type to grace the covers of magazines. They were an odd pair but worked together a majority of the time. Pure was careful with his words and Peaches would throat punch you with the truth.

"Joker, do you want to know? This is your choice," Peaches asked.

Dem's fingers tightened through his, and he took a deep breath as he debated whether he wanted to know or not. Two weeks passed since he'd come home. Dem and him seemed to be doing okay. An uncomfortable strain existed, but he knew he needed to earn Dem's trust. It was second nature for him to run to his shack, hop on his bike and head to parts unknown. No one ever worried about him or thought about where he went, yet now he had Dem.

"Why did y'all look in the first place?"

"Peaches came to me several weeks ago." Pure cleared his throat and slid the file in front of him. "I visited Pelter and checked cold cases. There were no body dumps that matched your mother's general description in anyway. Then I checked into long-term patients in mental health facilities, mainly voluntary check-ins. I focused on Georgia. Since your mother didn't have any sort of transportation or funds that we knew of. To be on the safe side, I widened the search to all neighboring states. For nineteen-eighty-seven I got forty-odd hits. I narrowed those down by calling and getting a description. I knocked it down to ten.

"I felt it necessary to ask your permission to continue. Peaches was adamant about finding her, but this is a choice you need to make. Thirty years has gone by, if one of the ten turns out to be Mary, then there's a reason she committed herself."

"Out of the ten, how many—"

Peaches answered when he couldn't finish the question. "All had suicide related incidences. One had a severe mental break. One has cases of Catatonia between brief lucid periods. There's one patient who's so adverse to touch that she has a psychotic break every time someone even passes too close to her. She's been deemed a danger to herself and others, her voluntary status was removed when she attacked one of the orderlies."

"The last one, do you have her file?"

Pure shifted and leaned back in his chair. "We don't have files, Joker, we asked some questions saying we worked for an investigative agency and a son was looking for his mother who disappeared around the time of admittance."

"And how did you get all this information," Dem asked.

"We may have used Joker's psychiatric report to outline possible symptoms and behaviors, to do a comparison of diagnoses." Peaches stared across the table at them.

"You thought since I was fucked up, she'd be similar?"

Peaches didn't pull any punches, "Yeah, that was the thought."

"I want to visit the last one."

"Joker, I don't think—"

"Fuck what you think, Pure, give me the address."

Joker knew it was her, the last one. If she was committed, it would explain why she hadn't come back. He couldn't be angry with her for leaving. He didn't know if that would change when he saw her. She had left him with Garnet knowing what the bastard was.

He snatched the paper up when Peaches slid it across the table. He stared at it, there was no name or physical description.

"Road trip?"

"Do I get to ride on your bike again?"

Dem seemed excited by the idea. He hadn't taken Dem out again for a ride even though he'd contemplated the idea a time or two. With the way things were between them since his last disappearance, he'd become increasingly careful which was unlike him.

"I think I can do that."

"I want a nice hotel, though."

He rolled his eyes. "Fine, no camping beside the road for you, all high-maintenance and shit."

"Damn right."

He couldn't miss the stares he received from Peaches and Pure. Peaches had known him longer, but Pure knew him almost as well. The sight of him holding someone's hand or catering to their whims had to be a stretch.

"You did just fine out at the shack."

"Road trip or not?"

"Road trip."

"Joker, I think you should wait until we know more." Peaches leaned her forearms on the table.

"What's waiting going to fucking get me? Nothing. If it's her, it's her."

"Joker, I just don't want you to get your hopes up and it not be her."

"No hopes here." That was partially true. He'd given up on the dreams of his mother coming back into his life decades ago, but if there was even a slight chance, he had to take it.

"Maybe you and Dem going away for a few days would be good for y'all."

Peaches' grin annoyed him to no end. She was as bad as Lily and Twitch with their incessant need to pair people off. Just because they were insanely happy didn't mean a happily ever after existed for everyone. Especially not him, he understood in his gut that he lived on borrowed time with Dem.

"Quit playing matchmaker," he ordered.

"I can do what I damn well please."

He released Dem's hand and stood, he didn't volunteer to help Dem. The man used his crutches to stand.

"Joker, promise me, if you need me don't hesitate to call like you did in Virginia."

"They didn't book me."

"Doesn't matter, call me."

He nodded then followed behind Dem toward the door. They could be maybe hours or a day away from finding his mother. Would she look at him and see Garnet? No matter how many times he looked in the mirror, he'd always seen Garnet. Garnet had gotten rid of all pictures of Mary; he didn't remember what his mother looked like. Was there even a bit of her in him?

Dem called his name, and he glanced toward him.

"We can wait, let Peaches and Pure dig a bit more."

"No, I want to know."

"Okay, we'll go."

They made their way to his truck in silence. He forced open the passenger side door and left Dem to get inside on his own. He liked Dem's independence. The man demanded basic things from him, a show of affection, the truth, but didn't attempt to cling or change him overnight. He doubted his personality and dysfunctions would change in the months or years to come. At almost forty, he was what he was, and he was comfortable with it.

The part of him that still bore some murky optimism wished he had years to come, but he wasn't ready yet to give in to that sliver of light he'd ruthlessly tried to extinguish.

16 That Was Frightening

The Waterford Institute was almost surreal. He'd never seen or assumed a mental facility would look like some country manor from fairy tales. The sweet scent of flowers clung to a gentle breeze. The lawn was impeccably kept, if not for the high fence and guardhouse at the gate, no one would assume. Jackson had been unusually quiet since they'd stopped for dinner and then found a room for the night.

The ride was amazing, but his body paid for it, and he'd been thankful Jackson hadn't insisted on pushing forward.

He turned to see Jackson staring up at the building.

"Mr. Webb, are you here about our Jane Doe?"

A pretty, petite woman in a doctor's jacket over a simple sundress approached. The woman didn't look old enough to be a doctor.

"Yes, I am."

"I'm Dr. Savari, I'm the Chief Facility Manager and only full-time doctor on staff here. Could we talk out here a moment? I've been in my office all morning."

He heard Jackson grumble, and he stepped forward.

"That's fine, I'm Demetri Urban, Jackson's partner."

Savari held out her hand with a bright smile on her face.

"Pleasure to meet you."

Her grip was firm and confident, and he liked the doctor. He wasn't so sure what Jackson thought of her, but the man still didn't like many people. He doubted his man liked him most of the time.

"Well, let me explain to you about Jane. I took over Waterford about a decade ago. It took me about a year, but I familiarized myself with every patient. Jane has been a challenge to say the least."

Savari motioned to a nearby group of benches.

They took a seat on one, and she sat facing them on the other.

"What challenges?"

It didn't seem Jackson was going to say much.

"From her lengthy file, she came to us and admitted herself, but wouldn't provide us with a name. Thirty years ago, standards of care were lax if I should say. That's neither here nor there. She didn't exhibit any violent tendencies, although, she was prone to self-harm. One such incident almost led to a supposed suicide attempt, but from reading her file, I didn't feel that was her intention.

"I've examined her at length over the years…she's covered in scars and most of them couldn't have come from being self-inflicted. I noted in her file that she was a victim of past torture and abuse. She speaks very little."

"But we were told her voluntary commitment became involuntary." Jackson remained stiff, and his hands were clenched on his thighs.

Dem knew better than to touch him right now. His man was on the edge.

"Yes, sad event and to be honest completely unnecessary to change her status. There was an orderly who took liberties—"

"You mean he fucked the patients."

Savari flinched. "Yes, in some cases the patients were catatonic. One night, he decided to go after Jane. She attempted to disembowel him with a knife from her dinner tray."

"What happened to him," Jackson growled.

"His improper behavior was discovered, he was fired and charged with several crimes. As far as I know, he's still in jail."

"Don't think about it, Jackson," he warned.

"I wasn't thinking anything."

"Don't make me warn Peaches. Please continue."

The doctor appeared more than a little uncomfortable.

"Yes, well, Jane has an almost psychotic aversion to touch, and for a woman of her stature, she's extremely strong. It takes several orderlies just to subdue her. Could I ask what the nature of your visit is? I'm interested for the fact that Jane, despite her reclusive behavior, she's a rather sweet woman and I would love for her to find her family. This isn't the place for her. Yes, we have a wonderful facility, and I've done my best to make our guests as comfortable as possible, though, I sense her issues stem from trauma more than any mental health issue that can be managed with meds."

"She's my mother."

"Oh, I should've known." Her face brightened. "Now that I've looked closer, you look remarkably like her."

"She was raped at thirteen, forced to marry the fucker, and I came along."

"As contrived as it sounds, I'm very sorry."

"I want to see her."

"Of course, I must warn you though, she doesn't take well to surprises. Go slow. Don't touch her. And whatever you do, don't come up behind her without announcing yourself."

It was inappropriate, but he smiled at the extremely familiar warnings. He was curious what a female version of Jackson would look like.

"Why weren't the authorities brought in when she committed herself," he asked.

"There's notes that an official investigation was requested, although, since there were no missing persons who fit her description, it was a fruitless inquiry. Please, follow me, she'll be in the back gardens about this time. She prefers her space and quiet."

She stood, and they followed.

"Will you two be joining her for lunch?"

He glanced at Jackson in time to catch the man's stiff nod.

He'd seen Jackson pissed off, cold and calculated, but the man was tense and devoid of emotion. He wondered if this was the man Jackson's friends knew him as, and he hadn't noticed it before.

"Very good, please, follow me."

He trailed behind the doctor as Jackson brought up the rear. It was a slow trip through the building, Savari stopped here and there to address patients she passed, even the ones who didn't acknowledge her. The place smelled clean. The interior bright and cheery, art graced the walls, and there even seemed to be groups of pictures of the patients at different holidays or functions. If this was all due to Savari, it appeared she'd done a great job.

Once they exited a back door and stopped on a stone patio, she stepped aside, and he noticed a small figure on a metal bench in the middle of a garden paradise. Her head tipped back, and her long, dark hair was braided down her back.

He turned to find Jackson's frozen in the doorway, so he moved to the side.

"Jackson, do you want me to go with you?"

"Yeah."

"I'll remain here until I know she's calm, then I'll leave you two to visit with her."

Jackson preceded him which told him the man wasn't all there. Yes, Jackson gave him his back on occasion, but not without Jackson preparing himself first. They took the ramp off the side of the patio and slowly approached.

Once they were within six feet of her, Jackson spoke.

"Mary?"

The woman gasped and jumped from the bench, she faced them with her hands clenched into tiny fists. At that distance, he noticed how fragile she appeared, but he didn't assume anything. Jackson and her weren't an exact match, but their eyes, hair, and features were remarkably similar.

"I thought you were fucking dead."

"Jack, you shouldn't be here," Mary's voice was high-pitched with fear, and she looked as if she was ready to run.

"I. Thought. You. Were. Fucking. Dead."

Each word enunciated with growing rage.

"You weren't supposed to find me."

Not exactly the mother-son reunion he expected.

"Does he know—"

"He's dead."

"When?" she asked.

He noticed her body started to relax and her fists unclenched.

"Twenty-two years ago, I killed him."

She backed up, and he wanted to reach out to Jackson, yet he knew it wouldn't be welcomed.

"Do you want to know why?"

He was thankful they'd left Killer at the motel, or they'd have one very pissed off dog on their hands when Joker ripped his sweatshirt and t-shirt over his head.

"Eight years I lived alone with that motherfucker, I endured every strike of his whip, every burning end of a cigar or cigarette, every, fucking, hit."

The early afternoon sun shined off every scar, played in the dips and bumps. His eyes burned, he'd seen them in muted light, caught sight of them in firelight and streetlight, but never full out in the daytime. He'd felt the sections where flesh was removed due to infection. Kissed every scar he was allowed to, but only the one night, the night where they'd had sex for the first and last time.

He flinched as Mary surged forward, and he waited for her to touch Jackson, but she didn't. Her small, shaking hands stayed an inch from Jackson's skin. They followed the contours, paused on the worst of them.

"Jack…" She cleared her throat. "I tried to kill him. I stood over him as he slept. I had the gun in my hand. My mind played out every time he touched me. The times he held me down, let his father hold me down. I cocked the gun, and he woke up. He used me the rest of the night, told me over and over he'd kill you."

"I read your journals."

She raised her hands to his face, again kept that minuscule amount of space between their skin.

"I loved you more than anything, even—"

"Even though I was—"

"There was nothing wrong with you, Jack. There was something wrong with Garnet and the other men in his family."

"I'm one of the men in the Webb family, so I'm just as fucked up as them."

"No way you were like them. If you read my diaries then you know I couldn't have loved you more."

"Then why?"

Mary and Jackson stood facing each other, not moving away or getting closer, just stared into each other's eyes. He didn't know why, but he felt Mary still loved her son. She'd thought she'd done the right thing, even if she hadn't said it yet.

"I went to my parents for help several times, and they always took me back. I begged them to take you. To keep you safe. They said it was the husband's right to discipline his wife. I wasn't a good woman. I seduced him, and I was paying for my sin."

"Why did you leave?"

"He thought he'd killed me that night. He dumped my body on the side of the road. I went to the Sheriff when I came to, and I was bleeding, his hand prints were still around my throat. Thorpe was going to take me back, on the way there, I opened the passenger side door, and I jumped. I ran."

"Then you committed yourself to some fucking loony bin."

"I didn't...don't have any skills, I barely remembered how to read. I stole clothes from a line behind some house and just walked, then hitchhiked. And I didn't know what I was going to do. Garnet kept me locked up. When we went to town, he was always with me. I had no friends other than you. You were everything. I fucked up, but…but I thought since you were a boy, his son, you'd be safe."

"I wasn't safe."

"Did he die painfully, Jack?"

"I beat him death, caved his head in."

"Good boy."

Dem stepped back at the vehemence in her voice. The coldness that came over her features that was so much like Jackson's, and that's when she touched Jackson. She lifted onto her toes and brushed a kiss to the corner of his mouth. Jackson didn't move, and he didn't even know if the man was breathing.

"What about your grandfather?"

"Drank himself to death a year after I got out of prison."

"He got off easy. I tried to burn his house down with him inside it. I failed every time I tried to do away with them."

"Well, isn't that just creepy," he said and took another step back.

He became the focus of Jackson and Mary. She tilted her head to the side and stared at him.

"Who is this," she asked her tone cold.

"This is Dem, my—"

"I'm his boyfriend."

Even through his discomfort, Jackson's glare was just too damn sexy. He had to be crazy.

"He's pretty, but I always thought—"

"I'd have a girlfriend?"

"No, I thought your boyfriend would be…not so like a model."

"He is pretty and high maintenance."

"I'm not high maintenance, says the man with a three-pound attack dog who wears clothes."

"She gets cold, you know that."

"Yeah, yeah, whatever your excuse."

"You're coming home," Jackson announced as he turned back to her. "We'll pack up your stuff."

"I can't."

"Why not?"

"What will I do? I don't have money, a place to live—"

"We'll figure something out."

"Jackson, you really need office help, I refuse to do that shit again. And there's room for another trailer out back of the garage if we clean out that one corner."

"I've lived here for—"

"Yeah, well, you don't need to be here. And everyone thinks I'm crazy anyway, one more crazy won't hurt nothing."

"I don't—"

"Shut up, you're coming."

"I'll go talk to the doctor while you two continue with your sweet reunion, now I have two of you. What the fuck was I thinking?"

"I told you to stay away, this ain't my fault."

He carefully turned and headed back to the ramp, then inside to find the doctor who disappeared. It was best if he handled the breakout because Jackson had no charm whatsoever. What had he been thinking when he thought moving to a small town in Georgia would be less excitement? It damn sure hadn't turned out that way.

17 She'll Gut Him With a Smile on her Face

"Joker," Pelter bellowed from the direction of his office.

He heard his name over the sound of his torch, and he jumped up and turned off the welding torch tossing it aside. He ran to his office to find Killer growling from her spot on his—his mother's desk, and Mary clenching a switchblade she liked to carry around.

"What the fuck is going on?"

"I came by to see you and—"

"I'll gut his oversized ass with a smile on my face."

"Mom, fuck, stand down. Damn, maybe I should get you a job with Linus."

It had taken them two weeks to spring Mary from Waterford. They were still leery of her tendency toward violence, and he hadn't worried too much, but for a tiny woman, she was homicidal as fuck.

"This is the Sheriff, Pelter, my mom Mary, Mary, Camden Pelter."

"He touches me again I take fingers."

"Charming, I see where you got your personality from," Pelter said with an odd smile.

Harper had come by and set Mary up with tons of new dresses, most concealed her scars, and Mary seemed to appreciate it. Killer had taken over trying to keep Mary calm. His dog trotted across the desk and yipped to be picked up. Luckily, Mary put the knife away and cuddled Killer.

He finally relaxed when she unarmed herself, and he turned to Pelter.

"What the fuck are you doing here?"

"Nice to see you too, Joker."

"I'm going to have my lunch, my son in law said he was making me something special. Killer goes with me," she muttered and skirted the edge of the room.

Pelter tracked Mary's movements until the woman was gone.

"I heard you found your mother, but she's not what I pictured."

"She's just settling in."

Mary wasn't settling in great, but she'd been at Waterford for thirty years. Used to a significant amount of structure. They'd get there, and she was getting along great with Dem. Which worried him a bit because he and the man hadn't talked much the last few weeks. Dem was keeping his distance. He didn't know what to do about it.

Asking Peaches would be a mistake. He definitely wouldn't go to Harper for advice. Best friend or not, they didn't talk about sex. He didn't talk about sex with anybody, but this really didn't have anything to do with sex, or at least he hoped. They'd slept in the same bed a few times although Dem was always gone by the time he woke up.

"How do you woo someone?"

Pelter shook his head and stared at him with a horrified expression.

"Why would you ask me that? Do I look I'm doing anything in the romance department?"

"If you let the twins pounce you, you'd have—"

"That is a non-issue. I'm not doing anything with Eric and Ellison."

"You know you're the only one who uses their real names."

"We're not talking about them. Since I don't think I'm getting out of this conversation, what the hell did you do to Dem?"

"I didn't do anything. It just hasn't been right since I disappeared the last time."

"Are you an idiot, man? You two are supposed to be in a relationship. You run every time things get to be too much. First, it was out to your shack. Second time, it was a solo road trip. He's probably wondering if you even want him."

"Of course I want him, who else would put up with my shit?"

"Is that the only reason you want him? Because he puts up with you?"

"No."

Pelter crossed his arms over his chest and leaned back on his desk.

"Miscommunication is for teenagers or twenty-somethings who don't know what they want out of life. You're a grown ass man, act like it."

"What if he doesn't want to deal with me?"

"Then ask him, and if so, move on and let him find someone else."

He didn't like the sound of that. Someone else touching Dem. He wanted Dem. It just wasn't—how could he subject Dem to him even for a short time?

"Didn't take you for being a jealous man."

"I'm not."

"Let me ask you this, out of thirty-eight years, have you ever met someone you cared for like you do Dem?"

"Only Harper, but that's different."

"Is he coming back to your place tonight?"

"I don't know, his overnight bag was gone when I got up."

"Do this, make something for dinner, call him and tell him you want to see him. When you have him there, tell him everything you're feeling, no matter how it sounds. Be honest. If you're honest, then everything should work out."

He nodded.

"Now, do me a favor."

"What?"

"Keep your mother out of my jail. I don't have enough cells to have two reserved for both of you."

"She's fine. Mary's just getting used to being free."

"I'm just saying."

He watched Pelter push away from the desk and waved as Pelter left.

He stood there with his hands on his hips, then pulled his phone from his pocket. He typed out a quick message to ask Dem to come back to the trailer after work. With that taken care of, he needed to head to the grocery store to find something for dinner. He needed to make Dem feel comfortable and important. That wasn't something he thought he could do. What did he know about making someone feel special?

###

The door of the trailer opened a little after five as he stood at the stove flipping steaks. He wasn't great in the kitchen, but he could do steaks.

He turned to track Dem's movements and realized the man hadn't brought in his bag. He tried to not let it get to him. He'd had all afternoon to go over his actions since they'd met. It was clear he hadn't done anything right with Dem. He took a deep breath.

"Hey, you're cooking."

"I don't know how good it will be."

He took the cast iron pan off the stove and put it into the pre-heated oven.

"What's going on, Jackson?"

"Sit…please."

Dem took a seat on the couch.

He shoved his hands into his pants pockets.

"I fucked up."

"Jackson, maybe this between us wasn't meant to be, I know I kind of came on a bit strong."

"No, shit, I'm fucking this up. I'm possessive of my things. My home. The shop. Killer. I've never had things other than those that were all mine. I've seen myself like Garnet for years. I wouldn't subject someone to me. To the possibility that I'm just like him."

"You're not like him. Yeah, you're a bit of an asshole, sometimes cold, but you're not abusive."

"Then what the fuck am I doing wrong?"

"You're not doing anything wrong. You just don't want to be with me, and that's fine."

"Bullshit," he spat out and knelt in front of Dem.

"Then why are you pulling away from me?"

"I don't want to hurt you like I did the night we—"

He dropped his head forward and then Dem's fingers combed through his hair.

"If you'd hurt me, do you think I would've stuck around? Before you answer, no, I wouldn't. You gave me just want I wanted. Everyone I've been with—"

He grumbled, and Dem laughed.

"You're cute when you're jealous. Jackson, look at me."

He took another deep breath, lifted his head and obeyed Dem. Dem was smiling and gently touched him. He couldn't interpret what the emotion he saw in Dem's gaze was. He'd never been one to be able to figure out what people were thinking or feeling. The clues people put out were a mystery to him.

"I can't say what's going to happen in a day, a year, even decades from now, but I know that I want this to work. I love your surly attitude. I even love your possessive nature because I understand it. You weren't ever allowed anything of your own, and what you do have, you take care of. When you need space, I'll give it to you, but you can't just run off when it gets to be too much. If you don't want me because I'm not physically perfect..."

He snorted. "You're sexy as fuck."

"Do you think I'm weaker because of my crutches?"

"Of course not. I barely pay attention to them."

"Another one of the reasons I like being with you. You don't try to help, and when you do, it has nothing to do with you seeing me as inferior."

"I'm the inferior one."

Dem leaned in and their mouths touched, the kiss was hard and possessive. He grabbed Dem's hips and tugged the man to the edge of the couch. He rubbed his cock against Dem's. Dem stiffened and moaned into his mouth. He broke the kiss and leaned his forehead against Dem's, it amazed him when he didn't flinch and his skin didn't crawl with the man touching him. He'd spent so many years on guard that he was quickly becoming addicted to Dem.

"I can't get over you let me touch you."

"I love touching you."

"You're staying the night."

"Question or order?"

"Order, we're having dinner and then going to bed, and you won't be gone when I wake up in the morning."

"I'm sorry, you've been having nightmares, and I know you're a little on edge after even if you don't remember them."

"No more, you stay."

"Okay, I don't work tomorrow. I'll need to call Gideon and Harper to let them know I won't be home."

"Do that." He kissed Dem, then stood. "I'll finish dinner."

He felt a bit lighter but knew they weren't out of the woods yet. He had a lot to make up for, and he was going to work his ass off. This was what he'd always secretly wanted; what he envied his friends for having. He quickly finished preparing dinner while Dem made his phone call and went to take a shower. One step at a time, one minute at a time, he had time.

18 Jackson Knew What He Liked

Two weeks of what came close to relationship bliss, except for Jackson's stubbornness but it wasn't like he hadn't been aware of it. They had gone on dates, rides, and spent time with Mary. She was settling in but was a little too quick to pull her knife. He loved the woman, though. Her life had been hell, to the point she'd locked herself away to stay safe.

There was one thing that annoyed him though. The man wouldn't go passed some make out sessions. He went to bed most nights with sexual frustration clawing at him.

"Your bed," he ordered Killer who was on the pillow next to him.

She stared at him, gave him her signature glare, but jumped from the bed. Killer still hated to share, but she was going to have to get over it. Jackson was his too.

He turned to the side and eased the sheet off Jackson. He shifted down the bed and moved to straddle Jackson's calves. The man's body to him was perfect. It didn't matter how many scars graced Jackson's skin. He kissed the ones he could reach, paid special attention to the ones on Jackson's hips, thighs and hidden by Jackson's pubes.

He inhaled Jackson's scent. Musky, spicy with hints of soap. He licked up the length of Jackson's cock, kissed the scars, and Jackson's hips lifted from the mattress. He grinned before he engulfed Jackson's dick and swallowed him completely. He groaned at the feel and taste of him. He bobbed his head as Jackson roughly gripped his hair. He played with Jackson's foreskin, sucked on it, nipped at it, and ran his tongue beneath it, gathering Jackson's flavor.

Opening his eyes, he glanced up to see the quick rise and fall of Jackson's chest, passed that to the man's heavy-lidded eyes, and Jackson's teeth were sunk into his lower lip. As he sucked Jackson's cock, he relished each moan, whimper and curse. The sound of his name broke as Jackson's upper body curled up and Jackson shifted his legs open.

The tug on his hair almost dislodged Jackson's dick, but he increased his suction and Jackson's stomach sucked in tight. He wasn't a match for Jackson's strength. As Jackson drew him near, Jackson sat up. The wet length of Jackson's cock notched with his between their stomachs.

Jackson kissed him rough, teeth and tongue, and Jackson's fingertips dug painfully into his ass. His thighs gripped Jackson's hips. Their movements were feverish and desperate. They couldn't seem to get close enough.

He rolled his head back as Jackson's fingers massaged his hole. A pleasurable pinch preceded several tips pushing inside. He twined his arms around Jackson's neck and rode his fingers, pushing his hips back as Jackson' removed his touch.

"No, come on, Jackson, don't tease."

Jackson pushed him back, and he glared at Jackson. The man was smirking at him.

Bastard.

"My needy boy. Why should I let you have this," Jackson asked as he stroked his hard, leaking cock.

He wanted that dick back in his mouth or better yet his ass. He jerked off so many times reliving the way Jackson had taken him last time. The soreness of his ass from being taken raw and rough. His high-pitched grunts still played in his head that accompanied each jab of Jackson's perfect cock into his ass.

It was the roughness and the out of control nature of Jackson's possession that he craved the most. He wasn't treated like he was less than because his body wasn't considered normal.

"You're cruel."

He reached for Jackson.

"No."

Jackson twisted to the side and pulled out the drawer, then he handed him the lube.

"Turn around, I want to watch you get your ass ready for me."

His face flushed and his hands tightened around the small bottle. Jackson helped him turn around to straddle his thighs backward. He slicked his fingers and brought his hand to his hole, then he thrust roughly inside with one finger.

Jackson palmed his cheeks and pulled them apart.

"You should see how fucking sexy that is. Show me how you want me to fuck you."

He leaned forward and placed his weight on his left hand, and he quickly worked up to four fingers. The slick, wet sounds joined Jackson's grunts behind him. He turned his head to find Jackson sweaty and flushed, Jackson jacked his cock in a brutal rhythm. He nearly came when Jackson placed his hand on his crease and thrust a thick thumb inside to join his fingers.

He tensed as he was grabbed and thrown to his back on the bed. Jackson's features were tense and sharp, his breathing was rough as if he couldn't catch his breath.

"You want it, don't you? Fuck, you should see yourself, all red and swollen, ready for my dick."

His legs were pushed back, then his arms were positioned to lock his ankles and his hands wrapped around the headboard.

"Don't fucking move."

He didn't say a word as Jackson sheathed himself with a condom and more lube. He swallowed hard as Jackson's knees came to rest beside his hips. He shifted until he was comfortable. Jackson didn't say anything, silently understood he needed to lay a certain way.

He watched as Jackson gripped the base of his latex covered cock and started to tease, shallowly pushing in and out. He tried to squeeze to keep Jackson inside, but that only made Jackson's smirk. If he didn't know Jackson better that expression would terrify him, but his cock only became harder.

A shout took him by surprise as Jackson slammed forward, and he bit his lip. Jackson withdrew slowly and repeated the quick, painful thrust. The force rocked him and the trailer. The sounds of pleasure coming from Jackson made it so much more than he expected. His body was flushed and slick, his heart beat a rhythm that was panic-inducing.

The fast and slow retreat and thrust grew to the point his hole was sore and his skin reddened from the slap of Jackson's hips against him.

Jackson's calloused hands wrapped around the front of his thighs and pulled him onto his cock. The man was focused on where their bodies joined. Jackson's muscles stood out harshly on his hairy body.

"I want to cum, touch—"

"You cum when I tell you."

Jackson pulled from him, and he released his legs to reach for Jackson. The man wouldn't be that cruel to leave him. Jackson's cock was red and his pubes slick with lube and sweat. It jerked with need.

His eyes widened as Jackson lubed his hand and forced Dem to his stomach. He buried his face in the pillow and screamed as Jackson fucked him with his fingers. The stretch was both heaven and hell. Jackson rammed into him pushing him closer to the edge, but he needed more. That more he didn't know—couldn't name.

"Scream for me. I want to hear how much you want it."

Jackson's voice was gruff and dangerous. He struggled until he could get his knees under him and slid them to the side.

He screamed and begged for more. Jackson leaned over him, kissed down the length of his spine to the top of his crease. His cock was painfully hard as it rubbed to the sheet under him, but still, he couldn't reach the orgasm he craved.

"Fuck me, fuck…"

That's when Jackson's fingers disappeared, and his cock was back where it belonged. He screamed and cried as Jackson used him. Jackson reached under him and jacked his cock in the same pace as Jackson's hips.

It was all he'd needed—Jackson's dick and the rough stroke of Jackson's hand. He clawed at the sheets and Jackson's hips slammed once more to his ass. His hips bowed upward, and he came. He ground against Jackson milking every second of the best orgasm he'd ever had.

Jackson's hand rested between his shoulder blades, and Jackson jerked from him. He listened to the sounds of Jackson jerking off behind him. He turned his head enough to watch, but he could only see Jackson's face.

"Tell me you're mine."

"Yours, Jackson."

"All mine, fuck, mine," Jackson spoke that single word repeatedly until he felt Jackson's hot seed on his ass.

The thick head of Jackson's cock pushed just above his hole, and he shivered at the trickle of seed.

Jackson laid on him and pushed their mouths together. The kiss was rough and possessive but also had a lazy pace. Jackson's arms held him close. He listened to the soft words, but couldn't make them out. He opened his eyes to find Jackson's lashes spiky with tears. They ran from the corners of Jackson's eyes. He didn't say a word, didn't draw attention to it, and he realized Jackson trembled.

Jackson's voice rose enough for him to hear, "Don't make me go away."

"Hey, shit." He worked until he could turn over and embrace Jackson. "Jackson, baby, what's wrong?"

"I should be gentle with you. Show you how much I—"

"How much what?" He wiped the tears and sweat from Jackson's face and hated Jackson wouldn't look at him.

"I love you. I think. I don't know what it's supposed to feel like."

"Then what do you assume it's supposed to feel like?"

This wasn't exactly the conversation he wanted to have after sex with his man, but communication was important. Especially when Jackson wasn't really that great about expressing any emotion other than anger or sarcasm.

"Like my friends are with their partners. They're always touching. They're happy when they see them. I've walked in on most of them fucking, and they were always gentle. I keep—"

"Don't, what happens in our bed is our business. Next time may be slow and gentle, or maybe it never will be. That's for us to decide. Not what others may find normal. I like that you're out of control."

"Do you think you'll love me one day?"

He hated his man was still insecure. Jackson still second guessed his every move and what he said. He knew Jackson would need time, a lot more time, and he was willing to give it to him. They had their agreements in place, and they were both happy with them. The one thing he wasn't happy about was they hadn't discussed their feelings as much as they should have. That had to change.

"Already done, I love you, it's new and we've been together a matter of months, but that doesn't change what I feel."

Jackson tucked his head under his chin, and he held Jackson close. Their bodies slowly cooled, and Jackson drew the sheet over them. He did love Jackson. Jackson survived so much and to be honest, it had come close to him never meeting Jackson.

He knew life with Jackson wasn't going to be easy, but it was worth it.

"Did you put Killer outside before you attacked me?"

"No, she's in her bed and maybe traumatized now."

"She'll get over it."

Jackson was heavy on top of him, and he loved it. Months ago, he wouldn't have anticipated he'd ever be this close to Jackson. Allowed to touch the angry and cranky man. Jackson just needed cuddles and plenty of love. He was willing to take care of both for however long they had together.

19 They Were in Trouble

Six months later...

"I leave you two alone for a week and what do I come back to find," Dem didn't sound pissed off, but his soon-to-be husband was normally a good-natured man.

The thought of proposing came to him several times, yet he shook it off. He needed Dem to be his partner—his husband. The perfect opportunity hadn't made itself known. Especially when shit like this kept happening.

"She started it," he yelled and pointed an accusing finger at his mother in the cell next to him.

"You're not blaming this one on me, Jackson."

He turned to find his mother pacing with Killer in the hoodie Mary stole from him. His dog spent equal time with both of them. Apparently, she was extremely attached to what she called her furry grandchild. Sometimes he wondered if she should be out of the hospital.

"What the hell happened?"

"Well, let me clear that up for you, Dem."

Fucking snitch. He glared at Pelter.

"I received a call four hours ago from Twitch saying they had trouble."

"Jackson," Dem groaned.

Why was it always him? He'd been good over the last six months, mostly, but Dem knew he was trying or at least he hoped Dem knew he was.

"No, this little fiasco was due to a certain pretty brunette."

He snorted and rolled from the cot, he stuck his arms through the bars and laced his fingers. When he'd heard a primal scream and turned to find Mary attached to some huge biker, his first instinct was to attack.

"Mary, what did you do?"

"I didn't do anything." She sniffled and turned away.

If he'd learned anything about his mother, he learned she had a con artist streak a mile wide. A sweet lady could get what she wanted with tears, well, as long as they didn't know her.

"Cut the shit, Mary, what happened?"

"Dem, she ain't talking, I've asked her I don't know how many times and Joker doesn't have any idea. All the witnesses said they heard this scream, and then she was wrapped around some biker four times her size."

"What did the biker do?"

"He didn't do shit from what I heard. He was actually holding his hands to the side as she was reaching for her—"

Dem sighed loudly. "Mary, what have we talked about?"

"He touched me."

"You were in a bar, people are going to touch you, brush against you, we've discussed this."

"Doesn't matter, he tried to rub on me."

"Bear didn't do anything of the sort. He wanted to buy you a drink."

Pelter sounded amused, and he knew the Sheriff had a weak spot for Mary even if he tried to hide it.

"Then get in my panties. I thought you took me to a gay bar." She huffed and looked at them accusingly.

"Mom, no mention of your granny panties, woman!"

"I don't wear granny panties, Twitch took me—"

"Mom!"

He glared at Dem and Pelter as the men laughed at him.

"When can we get out of here," he asked.

"Since the responsible adult is here, you two are free to go."

He stepped back as Pelter unlocked his cell door and he exited. He moved to Dem and wrapped his arms around his man. Dem had left to visit his parents and take care of cleaning out stuff he'd left at his ex's place and in a storage unit. He'd wanted to go along, but that hadn't been a good idea. They'd both agreed, and someone had to be there to watch Mary.

He'd thought he'd gotten his temper and rage from Garnet, but it turned out his mother was a bloodthirsty little thing.

"Mary, before I let you out you have to stop. You're safe here, and if you're not, then you come to me. I'll take care of it. You have to apologize to Bear."

"I'd rather stay in here."

"She'll apologize, I'll make sure of it," Dem said. "It's a good thing neither of us wants kids, your mother is bad enough."

"I think a kid would be better behaved."

He chuckled as Mary flipped them off and impatiently waited to be set free. Pelter sighed and unlocked her door. Mary turned sideways to exit. He understood her, so he didn't say much about her quirks.

"Come on, let's go home," Dem released him.

Mary followed behind grumbling the whole way.

"I ain't apologizing. I didn't do anything wrong, Dem, I didn't even get my knife out."

"Mary, this isn't up for discussion. We'll find the man, and you'll apologize."

"No, I ain't gonna."

"I'm not arguing with you. I'm rethinking this relationship, Jackson."

"The fuck you are." He wasn't having that shit.

"Can I trust you two to ride right home?"

Mary went straight to her bike he bought for her a month after she got out of Waterford. He'd have to thank the crew for bringing it out from Brawlers. She slammed her helmet on her head and without waiting, she started her bike, speeding toward home.

"What are we going to do about your mother?"

"She's fine, Dem, she doesn't understand."

"Not every man is like Garnet or that orderly. Maybe this guy is nice."

"Bear seems okay. He's King's uncle. I'll talk to him about it."

"I want Mary happy, but...I love your mother, but she's not adapting."

"I said she'll be fine."

"Okay, sorry."

"It's fine. I just don't know what to do. I get her...know what she went through."

"Enough about Mary, we need to discuss something, and I don't want you to be mad."

"That isn't the fucking way to start a conversation when you don't want someone to be mad."

"You shouldn't be mad, and really with you just getting out of jail, this seemed the appropriate time."

Dem produced a tiny black bag, and when he shook it, two rings fell into the man's palm.

"What the fuck is that?"

"Well, we're not exactly the most romantic couple, and I've been impatient. So, will you fucking marry me?"

He was shocked speechless. He looked from the circles of metal and then back at Dem. Dem looked nervous and chewed on his lower lip.

"Really?"

The man wanted to marry him. Spend the rest of his life with him—that's what marriage meant. Although it made him feel even more of an asshole, he was still waiting for Dem to get tired of him and find someone more…agreeable and sane. With the new development of being in charge of Mary, he assumed it would become too much sooner or later.

"Yes, really, my mother and I went to look at rings while I was in New York. She flew in just for that. I know I should've done this more…we're just not that kind of couple. Fucking say something."

"You want to marry me? Me, Joker Webb?"

"You're Jackson Webb, and yes, I want to marry every bastard inch of you, especially several inches I'm quite fond of."

He loved Dem's smile. The way Dem always knew when enough was enough. Dem didn't get angry when he needed space or the fact he still flinched sometimes, or he woke crying from nightmares. It was all fine, whatever he needed Dem gave him even if it was a few days to himself.

"Yes, but we have to do it soon before you change your mind. Let's talk to—"

"Jackson, Jackson, hold up." Dem held tight. "I want all our friends there. I want Gideon standing beside me and Harper beside you. I hear Lily is ordained to do weddings."

"An atheist minister, still weird, but she doesn't want anyone else to perform the ceremonies for her kids."

"So, you're going to marry me," Dem asked and held out one of the rings.

"Yes, I always wanted you to be mine."

Dem grabbed his bearded cheeks and pushed their mouths together, the kiss was slow to end. He held his man close. Wondered what the hell he'd done right in his life. Whatever it was, he wouldn't think too hard, and he'd get the man to marry him as soon as possible, so Dem didn't have a chance to change his mind. No matter what, Dem was his, and he would be thankful for it every day.

Epilogue: The Cranky Fucker was Going to Marry him

Dem needed a drink or several as he paced the living room of Gideon and Harper's house. A month passed since Jackson said yes to his weird and totally unromantic proposal, but he hadn't been able to wait. He'd had it all planned out, a dinner for the two of them, maybe a camping trip out to the shack. No, he'd blurted it out in front of the Sheriff's Department after picking up his boyfriend and Mary.

"You're gonna wear crutch marks in the nice carpet."

He turned to smile at Mary. She was dressed in a pretty pale pink dress. Her long hair was piled on top of her head in some elegant twist Twitch had done. She looked pretty and happy. She wasn't as gaunt as she was when they took her from the hospital.

"You're not rethinking marrying my son, right?"

"Absolutely not, you know this is where I started to fall for him."

"What?"

He motioned toward the picture on the mantle. "The first night I was here, I was looking around, and I saw that picture. He looked so sad and angry, but I had never seen a man as handsome as Jackson. I used to pull it down and put it on the coffee table to study him."

"My boy, I did what I thought was right. I know I fucked it up. I should've—"

"There's nothing you could've done, Mary. Do you really think Garnet would've let you take him?"

"No, but that doesn't make me any less guilty."

"I'm not going to say there's no reason to feel guilty. But what ifs are going to just make you miserable. I love Jackson. If things had been different, if you had come back for him, would I have ever had the chance to meet him? We can't say. You're here now."

"Your mother is making Jackson nervous."

"What's she doing?" He was terrified to know what Gretchen was doing to Jackson. Since she'd found out he wanted to ask Jackson to marry him, the woman was obsessed with having her future son-in-law love her.

"She keeps trying to hug him, and your dad, he's growling and trying to get her away from Jackson."

"Shit, maybe we should get this show on the road before Jackson turns into a runaway groom."

"Not going to happen, Dem, my boy loves you. He's possessive and he's sometimes an asshole, but there's no man who'd love you more."

"I know that. Want to walk me out?"

He held out his elbow, and he waited patiently for her to decide. He knew it would take a long time for her to be comfortable and to feel completely safe, but he would do everything in his power to make sure she got there.

"Yes, but *he's* out there."

He tried not to laugh and failed at her obvious horror. He didn't even have to ask who he was. Bear King had made it his mission in life to get Mary to go out with him. The man was really four times Mary's size. The one time he'd seen Bear near Mary, she barely came to his chest.

"Maybe give him a chance. I hear he's really sweet."

"No, I won't do it."

"That's fine, you don't have to do anything you don't want to. You always have the right to say no."

Mary nodded and then took his arm. They walked outside. His gaze instantly found Jackson wearing a suit. He'd never seen anyone as handsome. He descended the temporary ramp and carefully made his way across the yard.

Jackson's eyes locked with his and he smiled. That man was going to be his husband. He hadn't thought when he'd moved here he'd find the man he'd spend the rest of his life with, but Jackson was all his. Mary released his arm as he stopped in front of Jackson.

"I hate you."

"I hate you more."

His mouth spread into a wide smile as Jackson grinned at him. Jackson was everything he ever wanted and didn't know it. He'd forever be thankful to Gideon who offered him a place to stay. If not for that, he wouldn't have gotten his happily ever after. It might not be what everyone else assumed a fairy tale would be, but it was his, and no one would ever take that from him.

THE END

About the Author

By day, J.M. is an introverted cook hiding out in her kitchen in the middle of nowhere Ohio, by night and any free time she may have, she is a writer of mainly LGBTQ Fiction and Erotica. Although. she's equal opportunity when it comes to telling a story, she'll even write a bit of straight erotic romance when the mood strikes.

She has been writing for years in old notebooks. At the age of eight, she wrote the worst poem in the history of poetry, but it sparked her love for writing. She reads too much and loves to get lost in other worlds and her favorite stories have to include laughter and having the reader doing at least one double take. Thirty-something, forever restless she uses her stories to ground herself, and find her place of peace.

WHERE TO FIND J.M.
www.jmdabneyauthor.com